# THE
# SAGITTARIUS
# MYSTERIES
Revolver

Adrian Holland

Published by AMAZOLA

The right of Adrian Holland to be identified as the Author of the work has been asserted by him in accordance with the Copyright, Design and Patents Act 1988.

Copyright © Adrian Holland 2013

ISBN 978-1-909466-22-7

For further information please contact the official website at

www.amazolapublishing.com

A copy of this book is held at the British Library.

Cover design illustrations by Adrian Holland

I was very close to both of my parents who were my best friends, and I have lost count of the number of happy times we shared, and all of the creativity and laughter. Like my beloved father Joe, my mother Margaret was so special, and my total inspiration. I would therefore like to dedicate this book to their memory.

# Contents

# Introduction

The day had started normally for Brandon Sagittarius, Head of *Experimental* Department, British Intelligence (MI6) when he received a telephone call. It was no ordinary call, as he had been requested to attend a London health clinic to have an inoculation for something know as *Bat Flu*. The conversation had been strained, and the person on the other end seemed to have ulterior motives. Little did he realise at the time, just what sort of motives the caller had in mind!

The call was all part of a devious plan to remove him from his job, and to replace him with an imposter, someone who looked identical to him in virtually every way. Once replaced, he faced the prospect of being *terminated*, and if that prospect was not bad enough, the group behind it know as the *Organisation*, had plans to take over the entire country.

They sent one of their operatives to lure him into a trap, which would have succeeded if it has not been for his trusted friend and companion *Oracle*.

Fortunately, he managed to escape their clutches, and together with two others who Oracle had also managed to liberate from the conspiracy, fled to the comparative safety of his parent's home in the country.

The Organisation soon discovered their whereabouts, and sent an armed team after them, with orders to recover all of his highly classified research, before eliminating them all.

Somehow, they had managed to survive, and now he had to deal with the aftermath…

# One

The fragrance of freshly cut flowers drifted up from the clean bed linen, filling the room with the unmistakeable smell of lavender, as the sight of the inviting duvet filled his heart with joy.

It had been a long time since he had the pleasure of a good night's sleep, and Sagittarius could not wait to wrap himself in the cosiness of a familiar bed. It felt like heaven as he bathed in its comfort, snuggling down for a well earned rest.

There was nothing quite like it after a good meal and a hot shower. All of his troubles seemed to drift away on a wave of fabric conditioner, as he took a deep relaxing breath. It had been quite a few days, and now all that seemed to matter to him was the prospect of eight hours of uninterrupted sleep, which seemed like absolute bliss...

He was going to have to return to London tomorrow, although he was not thinking about that now. Nothing seemed to matter as he spread out, savouring the moment.

The quietness of his parents' home in Glastonbury was so different from the constant hustle and bustle of the big city, and letting his troubles drift away was going to be the order of the day.

He delicately reached over with his right hand, feeling for the gunshot wound in his left shoulder. It was still a bit tender to the touch, but it was miraculous how quickly it had healed, and if he was lucky, there would not even be a scar. He really did not mind one way or another, and it was true to say that at this moment in time nothing bothered him. It was partly relief at still being alive, and partly the homoeopathic medicine his mother Astrid had given to him. He had not a clue what it was, only the fact that in his opinion it was strong enough to knock out an elephant!

His father already had the repairs to their home well under way, and he was grateful that an *Agent* from one of the other Departments had arrived taking charge of the whole situation. That had come as a big relief to him, and between them, Sagittarius and his father had managed to keep the majority of their research secret. Questions had been asked, and skilfully dealt with, although he knew that it was far from over!

It was not going to be just a formality, and he doubted whether life would soon be getting back to normal. Casting an eye towards the bedside table, he could see *Oracle*, his *cyber rabbit* sitting on the recharging mat, twitching his whiskers occasionally as he tidied up a few loose ends. He was a marvellous companion, and had played quite a large part in their *adventure,* and containing virtually all of his memories, as well as thought patterns, in some ways they were more like twins.

Whether it was coincidence or just one of those things, but at the very moment he had that thought, the door opened slowly, as two identical faces peered around its white wooden surface. Sagittarius made out that he was asleep, as they crept into the room.

Gemini and Caprica, each wearing identical T-Shirts borrowed from his wardrobe stood at his bedside looking at him with love-sick puppy eyes. Sagittarius was stretched out in the middle of his double bed, and seizing their opportunity, they advanced in a pincer movement, gently slipping under the duvet on either side of him.

Sagittarius felt two sets of warm arms wrapping themselves around him, as Oracle twitched his whiskers again. He felt a sense of unease spreading throughout his body and his face flushed with embarrassment. They both had *tunnel vision* where he was concerned and now stuck to him like a pair of *limpets*. This was a very difficult situation and had to be handled with the utmost care, as they were both very sensitive young women. He felt flustered, losing the calm which he had been enjoying, not so much wondering what he was going to do with them, but more of a case of what they were going to do to him!

Sagittarius felt vulnerable, his privacy having been invaded. It had been bad enough having uninvited guests in his parents' home, now he had them in his own bed too!

Oracle picked up his thoughts as usual, understanding, as far as a *cyber rabbit* could, how he was feeling. Fortunately there was something that he could do about it, and so, unbeknown to them, he sent a signal to the nano robots inside their bodies. It was not exactly an on off switch, but it was sufficient to enable them to drift off into a deep sleep, much to the relief of his creator. Sagittarius was safe for now!


Two shocks of blonde hair stuck out of the duvet as Sagittarius awoke slowly from one of the most restful sleeps that he had ever had. He felt relaxed and contented, that was until he opened his eyes.

There, on either side of him, lay two very attractive young women. To most middle aged men, it would have been the ultimate fantasy, but not to him. Yes, it was very flattering, and he had to concede that they were both beautiful and infatuated

8

with him, it was just the fact that it all felt so wrong. They had been programmed to like him, and that was what was making him feel uncomfortable. Always the gentleman, he did not want to take advantage of the situation, fearing that he would be doing the wrong thing if he did.

What would happen if they regained their original personalities and became very distressed by what had taken place?

It was quite a dilemma!

The Organisation had a lot to answer for, and they were all victims in one way or another. He was very fortunate in having been able to recover from his ordeal, which was more than could be said for his sleeping companions. They both looked so young and innocent, even though they were in their twenties.

Whatever he did, he would have to proceed very carefully, feeling in some way responsible. It was not his fault, and if it had not been for his and his father's actions, he doubted whether they would be alive now. The blame lay squarely on the shoulders of the Organisation, and as he thought about it from the relative safety of his old bedroom, little did he realise that before long their paths would cross again...

# Two

A glorious morning awaited the occupants of *Freedom Farm*, who slept on oblivious to the wonders of the sunrise as it burst through the ancient arch of *Glastonbury Tor*, sitting high upon the distant hilltop, like some mythical guardian watching over them. The only one to have witnessed it was Oracle, who had peered out from behind the thick curtains hanging over the patio doors which led into the courtyard. Ever vigilant, his whiskers twitched as he scanned the area, just to make sure that there were no nasty surprises awaiting them. Yesterday had seen the arrival of the intruders, who had wreaked havoc in this normally quiet backwater.

Although just a cyber rabbit, he was beginning to develop what could be termed as *emotions*, and he was very concerned about everyone's safety. It had been a close run thing, and he was very grateful that they had all survived their encounter. The only casualty had been Sagittarius, who had been shot in the shoulder, and thanks to the nano robots within his body, the wound had been repaired and the bullet dissolved. It was not the physical scars that were his main concern, it was the mental anguish everyone had suffered.

Sensing that he was now awake, Oracle turned his attention to Sagittarius, who was deep in contemplation. He felt his thought patterns merging with his own, as the nano robots sent information to his main processor.

In one of the other bedrooms, *Big Jim*, Sagittarius's father was also beginning to stir, having, like Sagittarius's mother *Astrid*, had a lot on his mind. Big Jim had nearly been arrested for the attempted murder of his son, wife and their guests. In his dreams he was now facing a trial with the prospect of being sectioned and sent to a mental institute, where he would be spending the rest of his days. Astrid was also reliving the nightmare, as her home had been wrecked, her son shot and her husband nearly carted away like some deranged criminal. It was going to take them both a while to recover.

Oracle looked back into the bedroom, almost smiling to himself as Sagittarius lay there with two sets of arms tightly wrapped around him. He could sense how uncomfortable his creator felt with all of the unwanted attention. His mind had been altered by the foreign nano robots too, and by removing them, he had also removed a lot of his memories. Fortunately, Sagittarius had managed to download an incredible amount of information into his processor, and the friendly nano robots within his system had managed to replace the lost information.

Sagittarius knew that he had a lot to do today, and several major decisions to make. He longed to stay under the comfort of the warm duvet, and relaxed for a moment until he felt the pressure of two sets of arms holding tightly onto him as he tried to move. Looking from one side to the other, he could see two clumps of blonde hair, and his face flushed as he tried to remember what had happened last night. He breathed out a huge sigh of relief as he remembered that fortunately, it was only sleep!

Carefully, he removed the arms which were holding him down and eased himself out of the bed, as the two young women rolled onto their backs, still in a deep Oracle induced sleep. He could see a set of whiskers twitching and two eyes peering at him from the bedside cabinet. It was a welcome sight, and he smiled back at his companion and alter ego.

After a brief visit to the bathroom he returned, picking up the half empty bottle of water which sat on the other bedside table,

11

and slipping his glasses into the top pocket of his pyjama jacket, he calmly walked around the bed towards where Oracle was sitting. Picking him up gently, he eased the patio door open, sliding his feet into his slippers as he ventured outside.

The sunshine was bright, and he had to shield his eyes for a moment, until they adjusted themselves to the daylight. It was a scene of utter carnage, as the ornate patio garden lay in ruins with decapitated statues and shattered works of art strewn about everywhere. He felt a sense of great sadness that after the years of painstaking work his mother had put into it, it now resembled a scene more like a *war zone* than one which would have graced the pages of any glossy gardening magazine.

He cleared a few objects from the bench, and sat down placing Oracle on his lap and sighed deeply as he looked around. He instinctively felt his shoulder again, still marvelling at the healing process. Who would have thought that such a thing was possible, and yet it had healed completely, only leaving the faintest of scars.

He removed his hand, rubbing his fingers gently through Oracle's fur, realising how fortunate he was to still be alive. If the bullet would have been just a few inches nearer the centre of his chest, then he might not be sitting her today!

It was a nasty business, and how his life had changed in the last twenty four hours. This time yesterday he was on his way to work, with nothing more on his mind apart from a mound of paperwork. Now he had the Organisation to worry about, whoever they were?

The *Organisation,* however, was not the only thing on his mind, as he really felt for his parents, who he had involved in this situation. His father was strong and he knew that he would get over it, and his mother would come to terms with things too. The damage could be repaired, and the hastily boarded up kitchen door and windows would be replaced soon, as well as the storm shutters that had failed to protect them from the plastic explosives. The patio could be replanted, and artwork salvaged or replaced in time. His biggest dilemmas were now his job and his companions.

The Agent had left late last night, heading back to London with all of the details of what had happened, and when he made his report, Sagittarius knew that he would be in trouble. Some of his activities had been discovered, and being as he had been taking classified information home with him, he was now going to face a disciplinary hearing. Fortunately, the full extent of what he had been up to would not come out, and he thought that he had done just enough to cover up Oracle. Even so, he could still face a suspension, demotion and possibly even dismissal from the *Secret Service* altogether!

If ever they discovered the true nature of Oracle, then he would be confiscated and analysed, and he would never see his companion again. Sagittarius would be lost without him, and thirty years work would instantly disappear. He knew that he was not liked at the Department, and they would be only too glad to hold the *Court of Inquisition*. Things looked grim!

The other major problem he had to deal with was the two young women asleep in his bed. Everything they had with them including their clothes and personal effects, had been taken away for examination. The Department would leave no stone unturned in their investigation. The girls now had absolutely nothing of their own, with even their earrings being taken. His thoughts of them mingled with those of Oracle, who informed him of their mental condition.

The foreign nano robots had all been removed, and the consequences of their removal were that they had lost their entire memories. They had caused considerable damage, and being as their memories had not been backed up in the same way as his, they would not remember who they were, or anything about their lives. They were in effect *blank canvases*. They would still have their faculties, but would suffer from near total amnesia!

The young women's apartments would have been thoroughly cleansed by the Organisation, who would not leave a single trace for the Department to find, and it would be as if they had never been there at all. They had no memories of their families either, so they had no one, and nothing, just like two new born babies.

Sagittarius rested his chin on his free hand, whilst the other one continued to gently stroke Oracle.

Yesterday he had been a carefree bachelor, and today, well, things were a lot different!

It now looked as though he was about to join the ranks of the nineteenth century *Mormons*, as good as destined to have two wives!

What could he do?

He could not just abandon them, leaving them wrapped in a blanket on a church doorstep!

He was now all they had in the world, and just like new born babies, they had *imprinted* themselves upon him, and would be dependant on him for everything!

Sagittarius took a long swig of water, wishing that it was something stronger!

# Three

The sunlight was surprisingly warm this morning, and it looked as though they were in for a spell of warm weather, in contrast to the cool wind and rain showers of the previous few days. The United Kingdom has a temperate climate, which is hard to forecast as weather patterns are constantly changing; this is probably one of the reasons why it is a topic of polite conversation. The pleasant weather however, did little to lift his mood, as he sat stroking Oracle's fur. Sagittarius found it comforting, and although he was a *cyber rabbit*, being so lifelike, it just felt a natural thing to do. Comfort was one thing that he needed right now, and a sort with no added complications!

Sagittarius seemed to have the weight of the world on his shoulders as he contemplated the best course of action to take. Oracle was surprisingly quiet, as there was not much that he could do to help, apart from to keep monitoring everything. His sensors picked up movement within the buildings, and it was no surprise to him to hear the crunch of glass signalling Big Jim's impending arrival.

He was also awake early after a restless sleep, and Sagittarius smiled as he came sauntering out of one of the bedrooms, sitting down on the bench beside him.

"I couldn't sleep."

"Me neither."

Both father and son had been really unsettled by what had happened, and felt the need to talk.

"What's on your mind, Son?"

15

Sagittarius took a deep breath and explained what he had been thinking about. Big Jim nodded periodically, understanding his son's concerns.

"Well, they both seem like lovely girls, and you could do far worse."

That was not the point, it was the fact that there were two of them, they were now almost totally dependant on him, and the fact was that deep down he still did not completely trust them.

"Just give it time."

*Time*, was something that he did not have a plentiful supply of, as his other problem was what he was going to face later in the day when he went back to London.

"Do you think that I will face prosecution as I have stolen information and technology from the Department?"

Big Jim shook his head.

"I doubt it son, after all you have saved it from being compromised."

His father did have a point, although he instinctively knew that there would be trouble.

"How far do you think the Organisation stretches?"

Big Jim sighed.

"Everywhere!"

Both Sagittarius and Oracle looked at him.

"All of this has not just happened overnight you know, they have been working on things for generations. It's all *secret societies* and *bloodlines*."

16

Sagittarius felt another one of his father's conspiracy theories coming on.

"They already run half the planet, or near to it, and now they want to finally close the *net*."

Big Jim had some very strange ideas, and for someone blessed with a considerable intellect, it always made him out to appear to have crossed the fine line between brilliance and insanity!

"The Earth is wrapped in a magnetic field of circular lines which run from pole to pole. The *Ionosphere* is a giant electromagnetic-wave conductor, consisting of a layer of electrically charged particles acting as a shield from solar winds."

Big Jim was getting into his stride.

"Extremely low frequency or *Microwaves* referred to as *Schumann Resonance,* are identical to the frequency spectrum of our human brainwaves and can be tapped into by various means, such as transmitters or satellites. This *mind-control technology* was developed over fifty years ago. It can also be used to control weather patterns too. There is an enormous, invisible river consisting of water vapour which flows towards the poles in the lower atmosphere, as big as the Amazon. A massive flood can be created by *damming* these rivers, causing what could amount to a biblical flood."

Sagittarius looked up at the clear sky, feeling more than a little uncomfortable.

"It is also possible to use the web-like ionic structure to hypnotize people who are bathed in an artificial electromagnetic-wave. They can suffer symptoms such as

17

dizziness, chest pains, headaches, memory loss, stress, and schizophrenia."

Sagittarius looked at his father, wondering if he was suffering from something similar?

"With the new nano technology, there is no need to place a *chip* in people any more, and they can inject anyone with a vaccine such as flu shots, or tetanus. They often hear a *God* like voice telling them what to do; why do you think I had a layer of tin foil installed within these building to shield us from them."

Sagittarius breathed out as Oracle twitched his whiskers. At least it was better than his father wearing a *tin foil hat* around the house!

"Meditation can also be used to raise the mind and body's level of vibration - I learned all about that in my days in India."

Sagittarius began to think that perhaps he could do with a meditation himself, as his father was not really helping him to deal with his own problems. Although he was a wonderful person, Big Jim did have a habit of going off on a rather peculiar *tangent*.

"I know that you have your doubts, and like most people think that I am a little crazy, but you have to admit that what happened yesterday was not normal."

Big Jim did have a point, although Sagittarius still found the whole scenario so bizarre that he could not take it all that seriously. It was one thing to target the Department, and quite another to try and take over the entire world!

"Never mind son, you are safe here. Now, I don't know about you, but I could do with something to eat. Would you like me to fix us up some breakfast?"

Sagittarius nodded, he could not deal with all of this on an empty stomach!

Big Jim got up, moving his way towards the kitchen as Sagittarius took his glasses out of his pyjama jacket pocket. He was glad of their tints as the bright sunshine was straining his eyes. Oracle sat there impassively, bringing up a few conspiracy theory web sites, sensing what Sagittarius was thinking. They all seemed to be the same - more than a little *far-fetched* to his way of thinking. He then brought up the Local news headlines, searching to see if there were any reports about the break in.

*Government assures public that it has a sufficient stockpile of vaccines if the 'Bat Flu' epidemic turns into a 'pandemic'.*

*Independent business group launches latest communication satellite.*

*Anti Fracking protests gain momentum.*

*Man finds the image of Jesus on a supermarket potato after he claimed that he heard the voice of God in his head.*

Sagittarius thought that perhaps his father was not so crazy after all!

*Public spending review criticised by report*

*Somerset man arrested and charged with bigamy*

Sagittarius went pale, suddenly loosing his appetite…

# Four

The smell of a good vegetarian fry-up wafted out of the kitchen, as Big Jim hummed merrily to himself. He loved to eat, particularly breakfast, which was one of the factors accounting for his rather *rotund* figure. Sagittarius had been looking forward to it, although now he was having second thoughts!

The kitchen was a hive of activity when he entered, and although it had taken quite a battering by the plastic explosive, it was still operational, even though it looked a little worse for wear. The happy sounds and smells spread out into the hallway, and it was not long before Astrid appeared in a long flowing silken dressing gown. She looked a little fragile, but managed a smile as she worked her way through the muesli. His mother had a very healthy diet in contrast to her husband, which helped her to keep her figure.

It was hard to believe that such a young looking woman was Sagittarius's mother, and yet it would not be long before she reached sixty. She was not the only woman to have a very good figure however, as Gemini and Caprica poked their heads around the kitchen door. They both wore one of his large white T-Shirts, which had hung in his wardrobe. He had a dozen of them, as he always wore one under his white shirt.

Two sets of very shapely legs emerged walking over towards him, and their possessors pressed themselves against him kissing him on the cheek. His parents smiled at each other, finding it quite amusing. Even Oracle twitched his whiskers, having awakened them from a sound sleep. It was time to get started, as there was an impending trip back to London looming on the horizon.

After breakfast, Sagittarius showered and dressed in his usual black pinstriped suit, white shirt, red paisley cravat and shiny black Chelsea boots. He also had duplicate suits and boots in his wardrobe, along with the white shirts and T-Shirts.

The *girls* emerged, each wearing one of Astrid's borrowed long flowing summer dresses, much to his relief. He found it embarrassing seeing their near nakedness in front of his parents, although they had not taken the slightest bit of notice. It would not be fair on them or his mother to let them wear the borrowed items for very long, so they would have to pop into town to get something of their own.

Big Jim placed his car keys in Sagittarius's hand with a big beaming smile on his face. For some reason he had second guessed what the next few hours would bring, and again found the whole situation very amusing.

The girls had certainly *imprinted* themselves upon him, and looked at him with big *puppy* eyes, which reminded him of a documentary that he had seen a few months ago. It was all about animal behaviour, where an abandoned Lion cub had been rescued, and reared by a kindly soul. It had grown into a full sized adult, and yet still came for cuddles. Now his son had two Lionesses of his own, and he could see that they wanted far more than cuddles!

It did not take them long to reach Glastonbury, or to find a car parking space, as he knew his way around. The family had settled there after their travels, and in some ways it was still home to him.

He helped them down from the high seats, leaving them standing waiting for him as he purchased a ticket, returning and attaching it to the windscreen before locking the doors. Their

21

borrowed clothes did not seem to fit them properly, or the shoes which appeared to be a size too small. He realised that they would require a few items of their own, so he handed over his credit card. In his mind he expected them to purchase jeans and a top, and maybe some comfortable shoes. He nearly always used cash, but there was no point in trying to conceal his whereabouts today, as both the Department and the Organisation knew where he was.

An arm interlocked with both of his, as he escorted them towards the high street, raising the odd eyebrow from the locals. Oracle remained in the Land Rover, as Sagittarius planned to return once they had found a boutique. He was going to do a little research whilst they shopped, which he imagined would only take them about half an hour.

Kissing him on the cheek, they both disappeared with his credit card and he turned, walking back towards the car park.

With both of the *girls* safely deposited in the boutique, it was now time for him to concentrate on what he was going to do when he reached London. It was not only the problem of facing some sort of a disciplinary hearing, but also the fact that he still did not know whom to trust. For all he knew the whole Department, and maybe even the Government could be implicated, or even worse, have already been compromised!

Opening the passenger door, he climbed up into the seat, retrieving Oracle from his Gladstone bag. Looking like an old fashioned medical bag, it did give him the appearance of a doctor.

Oracle felt very comforting sitting on his lap, and he quickly established a connection, sending images onto the inside of his tinted glasses. The interface, together with all of the other equipment he had either *borrowed,* or *enhanced,* was going to be very hard to explain. There was also Oracle to consider, as keeping him secret was a priority. Was it going to be a wise decision returning to London?

If he failed to show up, then the Department would send someone after him, for even though things were not as they once were, they still had considerable resources at their disposal. If he went, then heaven knows what he would be walking into.

Oracle had been scanning the internet for clues about the Organisation, whose operatives had arrived in force the previous night. There were a few conspiracy theories but nothing tangible to go on, and the more that he thought about them, the less inclined he was to want to know. If his father was right, then it was going to be quite a mystery, and one which he was unsure as to whether he wished to solve.

It was a different Sagittarius to the one who had set off towards the clinic yesterday, and for the first time in years he felt a little vulnerable. Whatever those nano robots had done to him, had certainly left their mark. Feeling his shoulder, there was no physical scar, just a mental one.

Sagittarius also felt annoyed with himself, for he was showing weakness, which was so out of character, and the sooner he got back to his old self the better!

Time seemed to fly by as the warm sunshine eased him into a gentle sleep. His mind took him back to his youth when they had moved around a lot, living mostly out of a camper van. His parents were much younger in those days, and his father was slim and toned. They were real hippies, and the family travelled across France, all the way down to Turkey, and across the Middle East, ending up in Goa, India.

It was not until his mid teens when they returned to England, that his parents had finally started to settle down. It was hard to imagine that the unkempt child who wore the rainbow coloured clothes was the same smartly dressed man dozing in the Land Rover.

Nearly two hours had passed before Oracle finally woke him, and he had quite a shock when he looked out of the rear view mirror. He could see the *girls,* and instead of purchasing jeans and tops as he had hoped, they both wore identical short summer dresses, with low cleavages and little matching bolero cardigans. On their feet were sandals with a good heel, and they both had a matching handbag together with other shopping bags, which they carried in their free hands, as their arms were interlocked.

Oracle twitched his whiskers, picking up Sagittarius's thoughts as he sat there in disbelief. Heads turned as they sauntered past the locals, looking like they had both just stepped off the *catwalk.* They were really beautiful women, which did not help the situation, making him feel even more uncomfortable than ever as he climbed out to meet them.

He was greeted by hugs and kisses, and it was clear that they had dressed for him, and he could also see that they had had their hair done, and were fully made up too. I was almost too much for a man to bear…

# Five

Things were certainly *hotting up*, as the SIS Building loomed large on the horizon and the taxi brought them towards its white stone and green glass façade. Looking like a cross between a sandcastle and a power station, the futuristic building housing the *Secret Intelligence Service* head quarters was going to be the place where Sagittarius's whole future would be decided within the next few hours!

He felt quite tense as he sat there sandwiched between Gemini and Caprica, who were like a pair of *limpets*, determined not to let him out of their sight for a moment. Hours previously, after returning to *Freedom Farm*, he wished that he could have left them with his parents, but their presence had also been requested.

Even if it had not been, then he doubted that they would have agreed to let him go on his own. Travelling light, with probably the smallest summer dresses that he had ever seen, there was absolutely no way they were going to be left behind.

Their behaviour, although thankfully restrained, was however giving off ever increasing *hormonal* signals, which Sagittarius was finding increasing hard to resist. For some reason he did not fully trust them, although they had given him absolutely no signs of betrayal. It was something that he just had to work through, and he had spent the time whilst his father had driven them to Temple Meads station and during the train journey to Paddington contemplating it.

Now, as the black taxi cab pulled up near the main entrance, it was time to deal with his other main problem - a meeting with one of the *top brass*.

The taxi fare was expensive, as usual, and he was rapidly running out of cash, he was also in for quite a shock when he received his credit card statement!

Leaving them standing on the pavement, they all marvelled at the post modern design supposed to encompass many things such as *Art Deco*, a *Mayan Temple* and even something *Space Age*. Sagittarius had used the main entrance on several occasions, although there was more than one way to enter the building. Today was a formal occasion and his presence was going to be recorded at the main gatehouse. He was not sure whether his current rank would permit the admittance of his travelling companions, although he assumed, as their presence had been requested, that arrangements had already been made. So, it was with more than a little trepidation that he approached the man standing in the booth.

"Good Afternoon, Professor Brandon Sagittarius, Head of the Experimental Department."

He handed over his pass, which the man took, recognising him from their previous meetings. That was the thing about the professor, once seen, never forgotten. His unique style, not to mention his Gladstone bag, were things that no security guard could ever forget. Quite why he seemed to travel everywhere with a black rabbit was just as baffling as why he was now accompanied by two of the most attractive women that he had ever seen.

"Thank you, Professor."

The security guard handed him back his pass.

"I'm afraid that your companions will have to sign in here, and then when you get to the main entrance you will have to go through security."

That seemed fair enough, as they were walking through the main car park entrance. Security was a lot tighter here than the entrance via the Tailor's shop, and entering the building would require the *girls* to produce some identification.

This was not going to be easy, as everything they owned had already been confiscated, although having been interviewed by the agent sent to investigate the *break in*, they had been fingerprinted, retina scanned and a DNA sample taken, so he assumed that they would allow them into the building.

Sagittarius's hunch was proved right, as they already had their scans on record. There were a few raised eyebrows from security at the sight of them and Oracle, who was sitting quietly inside his Gladstone bag. He had managed to fool the sensors which scanned him, registering a normal black rabbit, and there was nothing more than a few cosmetics within the two young women's hand bags.

Sagittarius, being a little on the eccentric side, was the basis for some gossip, which had already spread around the building, and now there was going to be a whole lot more, as they would no doubt try to unravel just what he was doing with two such provocatively dressed companions!

They both kissed him on the cheek, leaving lipstick marks, as he was forced to leave them behind at the main reception. He then made his way to the lift, which would take him literally right to the *top* of the building.

The lift gave a customary *ping* as it signalled its arrival on the ground floor, and the doors slid open gently, revealing an empty compartment. Walking inside, Sagittarius waited for them to close and selected a floor right at the top of the building. The lift automatically began to rise, and as it did so,

27

he slipped his free hand into his inside pocket pulling out his fob watch as Oracle jammed the signal from the concealed camera within the roof.

The silver casing shone in the bright tube lights which illuminated the lift from the ceiling, as he looked at the clear white dial with the black Roman numerals. The hands approached three o'clock, which was when his disciplinary meeting was due to start. However, checking the time was not the only reason for producing his fob watch!

On the top there was a fastening, which formed a loop so that it could be attached to a chain that would normally have the other end secured to a gentleman's waistcoat. Sagittarius did not have a waistcoat, or use a chain, preferring to keep it in place via a Velcro strip which kept the jacket pocket sealed. He held the watch in his left hand, placing his Gladstone bag down on the floor for a moment as he gave the fastening a quick turn. He then gave it a little shake, and a fly slipped out onto the palm of his free hand.

He quickly pushed the fastening back in place, slipping the watch back into his inside pocket, as the fly came to life. Everything was done in less than a minute, and by the time the lift reached its designated floor the fly was buzzing around, before settling on one of the walls.

When the lift doors opened, Oracle allowed the camera signal to come back to life as both Sagittarius and the fly emerged into a corridor, with the fly venturing off on its own to complete its mission.

Oracle already had a visual link with it, and audio was on its way, as he sent it in search of information. It was vital that he

28

found out just what was going on, and more importantly, who had already been compromised within the *Security Service!*

It may have appeared that he had just been sitting there for hours, idly twitching his whiskers, but he had actually been involved in quite a complex if not incredible plan.

In coordination with Big Jim, they had isolated the frequency at which the foreign nano robots operated, and had managed to create the software program which could identify their signal. It was not easy to track them, but they had managed to create something which looked a little like a radar screen. Any foreign nano robot transmitting a signal within a certain area showed up within the program. It was in effect a *proximity sensor.*

Sagittarius's own nano robots gave off a signal too, and it was possible to identify anyone within a few feet from him who had been *compromised.* It seemed to be working well, as there were already several contacts showing up on the grid. The system was, however, limited, although they were working on expanding it to a greater distance. What they really needed was to gain satellite access, and that would open everything up.

The fly was acting not only as their eyes and ears on this floor, but it also relayed information about the foreign nano robot signals. Each signal operated on a slightly different range, so small that they all existed within the same frequency. Whoever had designed it certainly knew what they were doing, and that person went by the code name of *Dark Star.*

Contracted to provide technical assistance, the Organisation was relying upon the expert knowledge contained within the talented hacker's mind. They already had the system operational, but what they wanted was someone able to gain access to the database of all of those who worked within the Secret Service.

*Dark Star*, had already proved his worth, helping to amend and control the foreign nano robots, which was enough to convince them that whoever it was could be trusted.

Trust was something which they insisted upon, and anyone who failed to gain it, ended up regretting any deviation from the orders given. Ruthlessness was second nature to the ones who sat on the Organisation's controlling committee, and although the rewards were high, the slightest hint of betrayal would quickly lead to their unceremonious disposal!

There was a constant stream of information being received, and within it Sagittarius's progress was being monitored as he walked along the corridor to the prearranged meeting place.

The large oak door stood full of intimidation, marked with a plaque stating:

INTERVIEW ROOM ONE

This was the room that everyone within the Secret Service dreaded entering. It was akin to the *Headmaster's Office*, where you were sent to *explain yourself*. If you were sent here it meant trouble!

This was the first time that he had been here, and there were rumours that once inside, anyone who had been sent for would probably have the proverbial *book* thrown at them. It was where *Internal Security* would dissect any report made on a member of the *Service*, and discipline would be handed out. It could result in demotion, dismissal, or a custodial sentence, to be served in a maximum security prison...

# Six

Taking a deep breath, Sagittarius knocked on the door, opening it slowly as he walked inside. He was greeted by a smartly dressed woman, who was the *Personal Assistant* of the *Head of Internal Security.* She wore a sombre grey trouser suit. Although very smart, it lacked any colour, being deliberately chosen to denote the seriousness of her position.

The room was plain, white, with the usual desk, green lamp and filing cabinets, computer and coat stand. She had short brown hair and wore little make-up, being middle aged and quite stern in appearance.

"Professor Brandon Sagittarius!"

Sagittarius introduced himself, as she remained seated behind her standard oak desk. She did not offer him a seat, or rise to greet him.

"We have been expecting you, Professor."

That sounded ominous, and not the best of starts!

He remained standing as she deliberately tried to make him feel uncomfortable, letting an awkward pause develop, designed to unsettle him.

Sagittarius did not let it get to him, as he had used the same tactic himself. It was all about *mind games*, and establishing control, *softening him up*, before he faced what would amount to a *grilling!*

When she thought that he had waited long enough, she pressed a button on her telephone switchboard.

"I have Professor Sagittarius here for you, sir."

31

There was no reply from the other end, and they waited for a few moments, again all part of the unsettling process.

A well spoken voice eventually answered, which he could just about hear, as she was holding the receiver close to her ear.

"Proceed."

She then placed her receiver down, staring at him again. It was time for another awkward pause, to put him on the *back foot*.

"The Head will see you now!"

She eventually rose from behind her desk. Her words had been harsh, as was her manner, and it looked as though he was in for quite a *roasting*.

"If you would like to follow me."

She walked past him with barely an acknowledgement and gently knocked on the door.

"Enter."

The well spoken voice could be heard, and she opened the door, holding it for him as he walked past her.

"Thank you."

Sagittarius was well mannered as usual, and did not take any of her actions personally. She was just doing her job, and had to act in a certain way.

The room was also stark white, with nothing in it apart from a large wooden desk, and a single chair which sat in the middle. Two suited men sat behind the desk, which he presumed would be the *Head* and his *Deputy*, and behind them was a door and a large mirror, which stretched right across the wall. He suspected that it was *two-way*, and that there were others sitting behind it.

The men failed to rise, trying to intimidate him, although Sagittarius was having none of it.

They both looked very sombre, denoting the seriousness of the situation, and there was another one of the awkward pauses before either of them spoke.

"Please take a seat."

There was only the one chair available, and it was positioned in such a way, to make its occupant feel as uncomfortable as possible.

Sagittarius took his time, thinking that *two could play at this game.* He stared back at the men, *weighing them up* and trying to *psych them out.* There was a younger man, probably the *Deputy*, who was the one who had spoken, and an older one, probably the *Head*, who had remained silent. On the desk was a computer monitor and keyboard, and they each had a glass of water and a note pad.

By the look of things, he would not be surprised, if once he sat down, the lights would dim and a spotlight appear above his head!

Sagittarius moved slowly towards the chair, and when he was ready, he sat, placing his Gladstone bag by his feet. Inside, Oracle was observing everything through the material, as well as coordinating the fly and his other undertakings.

Although Sagittarius had never seen these men before, they did seem strangely familiar to him, and whoever they were, he had a very bad feeling about them.

The mental games continued as they made him wait again, although with Oracle transmitting him information, he was utilising the time they were giving him. He surmised that they had already made their decision and would pass on a final report. It looked like a *foregone conclusion,* but he realised that he had to *play the game.* What really interested him was who was behind the screen, and what they intended to do?

"Professor Sagittarius, you have been asked to attend this meeting on a disciplinary matter."

He knew that already, and had an idea that it would probably result in his dismissal!

"Now then Professor, we have read the report from one of our Agents and we would like to hear an account of what happened in your own words."

The younger suited man was doing all of the talking, and it looked as though they wanted to get straight down to business, which was not a bad thing. The sooner this was over, the better!

"However, before you start we would just like to point out that we are dismayed to find out that you have been taking classified information home with you, and that will result in certain disciplinary measures."

It was quite clear what they were trying to do, and he was right that his sentence had already been decided. He just stared at them, trying to give the impression that their intimidation was not working.

Looking directly into the eyes of the younger suited man, he spoke for the first time.

34

"Well, being as you are already aware that I was ordered to have a tetanus injection, which started everything off, I may as well get right down to the facts."

They stared blankly at him as he continued.

"From what I have been able to deduce, whoever is behind this has taken my astrological name and used it as a code word. It is no coincidence that the two young women I have brought with me today are called Gemini and Caprica."

They had a computer screen in front of them, which showed an image of the girls sitting quietly in reception.

"Now, as we know, there are twelve signs of the zodiac, and having already used three, that leaves the remaining nine."

He decided to hit them with the facts in the direct, uncompromising manner everyone had got used to. He had changed however, and the foreign nano robots had softened him, which was something that was making this more difficult than it would normally have been.

"For a start, I had a hunch that there were two people behind the original telephone conversation, which sent me to the Inner Vision clinic, where a *Doctor Crawley* injected me. I also had a hunch that they might be in one of those *Gentleman's Clubs*."

Sagittarius was being clever - a bit too clever for the men, who for the first time began to look uncomfortable. He was now *turning the tables* on them, and it was obvious that they were also probably members of a similar establishment, judging by the look of them. The younger man was greying and of small stature, whilst the other was older and balding. They both wore sombre suits, and he could visualise them sitting in

*Chesterfield* chairs drinking spirits and discussing things in a booth.

"I would therefore suggest that they would probably use the code names of *Aries* - strong willed and a risk taker, and *Scorpio* - big and bold with a nasty sting in the tail."

Big Jim had used that analysis, and he was almost accusing in the way that he said it.

"Referring to the men who broke into my home, together with my *doppelgänger*, I would suggest that their leader would be *Taurus* - strong and stubborn, with great stamina, accompanied by *Aquarius* - intelligent and rebellious. I felt that Doctor Crawley was likely to be *Pisces,* as there was defiantly something *fishy* about him!"

Sagittarius repeated his father's bad joke, which seemed to fall on *deaf ears*.

"I must admit that it was a bit perturbing finding out that there was a duplicate of me walking about, and even more concerning when I realised that I was about to be replaced by him!"

They sat impassively as he continued.

"Logically, that would leave us with *Cancer, Leo, Virgo,* and *Libra.* However, there is a thirteenth sign of the zodiac, one which is seldom used, *Arachnid* - spinning a web of intrigue, and ready to pounce on any unsuspecting soul who gets caught up in his plans. I would not mind betting that that is the person in overall charge!"

Again, there was no reaction from them.

"I doubt that they would have wasted any more resources on duplicates. The only reason they duplicated me was so that they could gain access to my work, not to mention infiltrate the Department. They also needed a backup of Gemini, just in case anything went wrong with her, as she was their main contact."

There was silence, and an uncomfortable one at that, which he knew were their tactics, designed to unsettle him and get him to divulge more information than he wished to do. Sagittarius was not going to fall for that one, as he was using the same tactic himself.

Eventually the younger man spoke, breaking the silence.

"We have read the report, and are thankful for your concise appraisal. We know the circumstances, namely that you were lured to the Inner Vision clinic on the pretence of having a tetanus injection, accosted and injected there. Also that you met up with a young woman who befriended you, and that you returned to your home, where you encountered what you refer to as your *doppelgänger*. From there you escaped the clutches of two other men and journeyed to your parent's home just outside Glastonbury. There a *break in* took place, which resulted in the involvement of members of the Tactical Fire Arms unit. We also know that you were shot, and that your wound miraculously healed - quite a tale would you not say, Professor!"

Sagittarius nodded.

"We know the circumstances Professor, but what we are really interested in, is how you healed so quickly, and what you have taken from the Department."

Sagittarius got the distinct impression that they were not the slightest bit concerned about him or his family, or indeed the

37

breach of security. It was also obvious to him that they lacked any real emotion.

"I do not know what you are referring to."

He decided to deny everything, as the onus was on them to prove that he had indeed *taken* anything.

"You know perfectly well what we are referring too!"

Sagittarius refused to take the bait.

"Can you be more specific?"

The men looked at each other before the younger man pressed on with his questioning.

"Nano technology."

Sagittarius put on an innocent look.

"We were conducting research within the Department, although it is still in its infancy."

It looked as though the men were beginning to get a little frustrated, which was what he was attempting to do - *reverse psychology!*

"Come now Professor, we all know that you are quite an expert on the subject."

He was, far more than they knew, but he was not going to reveal anything to them.

"You flatter me!"

There were indeed many experts within the Department, and someone outside it too, who had created his own nano robots which had been not only been injected into him, but also into the others that he had encountered.

"How do you explain how quickly you healed?"

Sagittarius continued to look innocent.

"I live a very healthy life, and am blessed with a healthy immune system too."

They looked suitably unimpressed by his statement.

"A most remarkable one, if the reports are to be believed."

Sagittarius smiled.

"So you deny taking any research out of the Department."

He looked straight at them.

"I have nothing further to add."

He sat there stubbornly, with his arms crossed. There was no way that he was going to incriminate himself, and from the expression on his face, they realised that there was nothing else he was going to say.

"I see!"

The two men looked at each other.

"Well, in that case you leave us with very little choice."

The older man pressed a concealed buzzer under his desk, and within a few moments the door opened behind them, and out walked *Taurus* holding a revolver...

# Seven

The shiny steel of the gun caught the glare of the strip lights which shone down from above, and Sagittarius could see that it was not a regular service revolver. He was no expert on guns, but for a start it was not fitted with a silencer. If he did not know any better, then he would have assumed that it had somehow been purchased off some *underworld* arms dealer. It certainly looked as though it could do considerable damage, and that the Organisation's connections knew no bounds.

It was almost like déjà vu as Sagittarius faced the prospect of being shot by Taurus again, and this time it would make a considerable noise, not to mention damage. Last time he had been lucky as the bullet had entered his shoulder. This time however, from the look on his face, it appeared that he may well shoot to kill!

In some ways it was quite surreal, as it proved without any reasonable doubt that the Department had indeed been *compromised.* Everything also seemed to be moving in slow motion as Taurus stood there, revolver in hand, with his finger poised over the trigger.

"I have a feeling that you will now decide to cooperate."

The younger suited man nodded towards Taurus.

"…and if you think that anyone will be coming to your aid, then think again!"

The warning reverberated around Sagittarius's mind, as he sat there staring at him, and then back towards Taurus.

"If a shot is heard, then you will be found, having been overpowered. With your already eccentric behaviour, it will be assumed that you, like your father, have finally lost the proverbial *plot*!"

It certainly was déjà vu!

"Taurus here, will be credited with stopping your attempts to assassinate one, or indeed both of us. Naturally, you will have been shot and indeed killed in the resulting struggle."

Sagittarius frowned.

"So, it is up to you whether or not you wish to talk."

The word *talk* seemed to trigger something off in his mind, as the younger suited man's voice suddenly became familiar. Sagittarius could have sworn that he had heard those particular *public school* tones before, and as he briefly closed his eyes it suddenly came to him. If he did not know any better then he could have sworn that they were the ones he had heard on the other end of the telephone line, when he had been ordered to attend the *Inner Vision clinic*. The more he thought about it, the more it began to make sense to him. Opening his eyes, he could just imagine both of the suited men sitting in *Chesterfield* chairs in a *Gentlemen's Club*.

The plot began to thicken!

So, if they were the two men he thought they were, and there was no reason to doubt that they were not, then it also meant that it left only one other possible scenario - the Metropolitan Police Force had also been compromised!

The call to them, and the information given, should have resulted in their arrest. The Organisation seemed to be everywhere, and he began to wonder just how far it stretched?

Things looked grim, as a smirk spread across the men's faces, for they appeared to be holding all of the proverbial *cards*. Taurus, rather than smirking, seemed to be out for revenge, and had a really evil look on his face. He had already shot Sagittarius once, and by the look of him, he would enjoy shooting him again!

"I think that it is about time you started to cooperate."

The younger man spoke, looking in Taurus's direction.

"It also looks as if *Taurus* here wishes to take care of some *unfinished business* too!"

Sagittarius kept his cool, not rising to the goading that was taking place. He was already thinking of trying to overpower them, and maybe Oracle would be able to fire his taser?

Any thoughts of action quickly subsided as the door behind the men opened again, and out walked his *doppelgänger*.

"Good afternoon, Professor."

It was uncanny, as he not only looked identical, but also sounded identical too. He was dressed in a black pinstriped suit, white shirt, red paisley cravat, and Chelsea boots. They were similar body types, with almost identical features, even down to the stubble and swept back black wavy hair. It was almost like looking into a mirror, and it was the first time that he had managed to get a really good look at him. Last time, he had been lying unconscious on the floor, something which he was no doubt still brooding over.

"I would love to stay and chat, but unfortunately I have a prior engagement."

He walked calmly towards him, as Taurus covered his movements.

"I have a rendezvous with two rather attractive young ladies."

Sagittarius frowned.

"Perks of the job, what!"

He thought about Gemini and Caprica sitting there waiting for him. So far he had been very careful not to take advantage of their infatuation with him, and now it looked as though this imposter was about to do what he had refrained from doing!

Sagittarius felt a heavy weight in his stomach, not only feeling responsible for them, but also deeply worried about them too. They were both still vulnerable after the effects of the foreign nano robots, and now their vulnerabilities were going to be exposed, as they would naturally assume that this imposter was actually him!

The younger of the two suited men spoke again.

"Carry on Mr Sagittarius, and take that dammed *rabbit* with you."

The real Sagittarius looked on as the imposter bent down taking hold of his Gladstone bag. Inside sat Oracle, and he frowned again as his trusted friend and companion was unceremoniously removed. A mixture of frustration and anger ran through his veins, as he watched them leave. He was now totally alone, having to face whatever they had in store for him on his own.

Oracle sat there impassively as he felt the Gladstone bag rise. This was one of the many scenarios that he had considered on their journey to London, and even though he was quite capable of acting, he decided to let things play out, as he needed to gain further information.

The other Sagittarius left the room, walking through the adjoining office, smiling at the Personal Assistant. She just looked back as he walked past her and out into the corridor. Within a few moments he was entering the lift compartment, about to travel down to his waiting guests.

Oracle could see him through the fabric of the bag, and although it may have looked as though he was not going to do anything, he had more than one trick up his proverbial *sleeve*.

He still had the *fly* for one thing, which had now settled high on the wall above where Sagittarius was sitting. It not only transmitted a wealth of information, but was also helping to track the signal, generated by the foreign nano robots.

The lift descended slowly towards the ground floor, as the numbers indicating the floor level lit up one after another, as they counted down. The other Sagittarius felt rather pleased with himself, and his smile increased as the lift came to a halt.

The reception area was quite busy, as people came and went. Everyone was scanned and checked by security, having to pass through the barrier between the outside doors and the rest of the building. It was divided into three parts, the reception desk, the waiting area, and the lift and stairs.

The other Sagittarius calmly walked out of the lift, holding his Gladstone bag, and looking for all the world like the *Professor*, and the *Head of Experimental Department*. To the untrained eye, there was no way of telling this imposter from the real professor, and they even shared many of the same mannerisms and memories, courtesy of the nano technology swimming around within his body.

44

Gemini and Caprica saw him approach and both got up moving towards him. They had not expected to see him so quickly, and had been waiting to be questioned themselves. In their minds they could see themselves having to explain what they had done over the past few months, but unfortunately their minds were complete blanks. The only thing that they could think of was the man walking slowly towards them with a big smile on his face.

He hugged and kissed them both passionately, much to the astonishment of the other people in reception. This was not the sort of behaviour expected by anyone working for *British Intelligence*, particularly by a *Head of Department*.

"Everything is over, and we are free to leave."

His words were greeted with a mixture of relief and excitement, as not only had they been saved from having to give evidence, but it also meant that they now had him all to themselves!

They clung onto him excitedly before reaching down to pick up their handbags, and then, as they linked arms with him, they all made their way towards the security check.

The machine bleeped the *all clear* as the security guards checked their bags, which indicated that they were not concealing anything more suspicious than a large black rabbit!

The security man bade them a *good afternoon*, which was reciprocated, and then followed by a cheery wave. Oracle had managed to fool the security system again, and the other Sagittarius had also fooled it too. He was such a good copy that it could not tell him apart from the real professor.

Back inside the room, there was no movement, apart from the characters on the computer screen which sat on the desk in front of the two men. From a secret location neither of them had the first idea of where, *Dark Star*, the shadowy figure confirmed that the observational link was working, and that the next part of the plan had commenced.

The signal had been ingeniously bounced off several fictitious accounts and there was absolutely no way of tracing exactly where it originated from. The men believed that whoever this *Dark Star* really was, he had a location somewhere within the British Isles, as they knew that any communication went via the internet or a Post office address, which again had many aliases.

He, or indeed she, could be anyone, anywhere, and all that they, and the other members of the Organisation knew, was that Dark Star was a high level computer hacker recruited via an advert in a computer magazine, or was even this assumption correct?

The Organisation had many tentacles, reaching into big business and various governments and security apparatus, but even they had no way of tracing where the signals were coming from, and more importantly, who was sending them?

The only important thing was the fact that whoever it was delivered what they asked for on time, with no questions asked. Payment was always made via an elaborate series of untraceable offshore accounts, which again left no discernible trail to follow.

There was a bug inside the room somewhere, which sent video and audio signals, so that *Dark Star* knew exactly what was going on. Detection and removal of the bug would result in the loss of the contract, something which the Organisation would strongly object too. This shadowy figure formed a large part of this current scenario, and everything was now going according to plan. The minor setback at *Freedom Farm* had been overcome, and they were now ready to close the proverbial *net*.

Sagittarius sat with his hands on the arms of the chair, which was quite bulky, being made of steel, with a padded seat, arms and back. It was comfortable, although a little over engineered for a mere office seat. It had occurred to him that there was something not quite right about it, and all of a sudden, arm and leg restraints shot out of it, gripping him tightly. He tried to move, but discovered that it was also bolted to the floor, and everything had been done so discreetly that it was almost impossible to detect.

All three men smirked as the door opened again, and out walked Doctor Crawley.

The Doctor wore a white coat, and still had that creepy air about him which sent a shiver down Sagittarius's spine. He had been here before, and it was with no surprise that he produced a syringe from his pocket. Sagittarius had a funny feeling that he knew what it contained, but could do nothing as he approached sticking it in his arm, and injecting him with what he suspected was another dose of foreign nano robots!

# Eight

The sharp prick of the needle was nothing compared to the sudden rush of foreign nano robots that flowed into his blood stream, dispersing almost instantaneously. Sagittarius cursed under his breath, realising that he had fallen right into their hands. How could he have missed the tell-tale signs of the unusual chair?

Now that he thought about it, it was obvious that they were not going to just let him sit there, denying all knowledge of what he had actually done. He was most indignant at the invasion of his body, which last time had rendered him unconscious and eventually resulted in the loss of practically all of his memories. He had only been saved by Oracle, who was now getting further away every second, and this time there was no one who was going to come to his aid!

Indignity was one thing, but plain stupidity was another. How could he have let this happen?

It was Interview Room One after all!

Everything had been meticulously planned, which was the way in which the Organisation liked to operate. They now had their man, and a duplicate posing as him, and it seemed as though it was now *checkmate*!

The Sagittarius of only a few days ago would never have been so careless; maybe it was time to leave the service?

The thought had crossed his mind, although now that the Organisation had targeted him, there would be no hiding place. Once they had someone in their sights, they would not give in until that person had either been compromised or eliminated!

He could feel the foreign nano robots working their way through his blood stream, and a cold shiver followed them up his spine towards his brain.

The men just sat there, waiting for the nano robots to take effect, and if it was going to be like last time, then that would not be very long!

In only a few short minutes Sagittarius felt his mind beginning to cloud, and although he fought to resist, he realised that resistance was futile!

When they thought that they had waited long enough, the younger of the *suits* began to speak. He was the one who always did all of the talking, with the other, older man just observing. It was as though he was the one who was actually in charge, or could he just be the observer who reported to his next in command?

It did not seem to matter who was in charge, as there was nothing that Sagittarius could do about it. Taurus was still standing by them, ready to shoot him if the order was given. To make matters worse, he felt as though his mouth had a mind of its own as it started to open.

"Now, Professor, I will ask you again what exactly did you take from the Department, and what have you been secretly working on?"

Sagittarius's lips moved, about to betray him, and there was not a thing that he could do to stop them as a word began to form in his mouth. This was a very odd sensation, as it felt as though he was now a puppet, and that there was somebody literally *pulling his strings*. Still fighting against it, he battled to regain control, but it was too late.

49

"Nano technology."

The words struggled out, and he felt terrible.

"Now, that is more like it, Professor."

The younger suited man seemed very pleased with himself.

"We suspected as much."

Sagittarius was determined not to give them any more information, as he tried to grit his teeth. It was not easy, as he not only had to battle against his own body, but also had Taurus's revolver pointing at him, and the Doctor waiting to administer another injection. Sagittarius had never felt so alone!

He may have felt like that, but he was not completely on his own, for sitting on the wall above him was the fly. It was transmitting everything to Oracle, via the transmitter embedded in his fob watch.

Oracle was still sitting in his Gladstone bag, being carried across the car park by the other Sagittarius, as they all made their way towards the main gate. The security guard inside recognised them from before and they were waved through. The other Sagittarius gave a warm smile, not only for the security guard, but also for himself, as he was now in the clear.

Afternoon was rapidly leading into early evening, and he was determined to make the most of this opportunity. It did his ego a power of good to be accompanied by two beautiful women, and even though he was a duplicate, he still retained certain elements of his own character.

With warm sunshine filtering down from the clear blue sky, he appreciated the looks he obtained from passers by as he strode along the pavement with Gemini on one arm and Caprica on the other. In his mind he had already decided how the evening would progress, and the first thing that he was going to do was to prepare them for what was to come. This he was going to achieve with the aid of a wine bar, which was only a little way further down the road.

When he suggested going for a *little drink*, there were no objections from the two young women. They were in the mood to celebrate, as it looked as though everything was now over.

The other Sagittarius opened the door for them, and they walked into the air conditioned bar, which had an air of sophistication about it. The décor was quite modern, with expensive looking fittings which gave it a continental style. He guided them towards a table near the window, helping them into their seats in the same manner the real professor would have done. They could not tell the difference, and a mixture of excitement and relief clouded their judgement.

The barman left what he was doing as the other Sagittarius walked towards the bar and, looking at his Gladstone bag sitting on the floor by the table, he naturally assumed as most people would, that he was involved in the medical profession.

"What can I get you, Doctor?"

The other Sagittarius applied the charm.

"Oh, there is no escaping what I do whenever I take my bag with me."

The barman felt pleased with himself, not realising that the bag actually contained a cyber rabbit!

"I would like to order a bottle of *Chardonnay* and three glasses please.

51

The barman nodded, leaving him for a moment as he turned to open the refrigerator, which held the bottles of chilling wine. The other Sagittarius briefly looked at him, before being distracted by the television, which sat on a bracket on the side wall. It was tuned into one of the twenty four hour news channels, and the newscaster was half way through a story about the stock market. In the top left hand corner, some red figures were being displayed, indicating that things were not going too well for investors.

*Today's fall is one of the worst that we have seen in years, with the FTSE 100 falling over 200 points. The Dow Jones has fared little better, and is also down a similar amount. Experts put the falls down to the increasing uncertainty about the so called 'Bat Flu' epidemic. Although the Government insist that they have sufficient vaccines to go round, they have been criticised by the way they have allocated them. The Opposition Health Spokesperson accused them of being elitist, as a government leak seems to confirm the rumour that so called 'professional people' will receive the vaccines first.*

The barman regained his attention as he placed the opened bottle down before reaching for three glasses.

"It's all doom and gloom!"

The other Sagittarius smiled.

"Well at least the sun is shining, which makes a pleasant change for London."

It was now the barman's turn to smile, although both smiles quickly evaporated, as the newscaster moved on to her next report.

*Weather experts are predicting heavy rain and high winds to bring unusually stormy weather as a deepening low pressure system sweeps across the Atlantic. We would usually only expect such a deep low to affect us in the autumn or winter, and experts are blaming global warming.*

"Bloomin typical!"

The barman placed the glasses down on a tray with the bottle as the other Sagittarius handed him a twenty pound note.

"Keep the change!"

That lifted his mood and he gratefully accepted it.

Picking up the tray he walked back towards the two young women who eagerly awaited the wine's arrival. He poured them both a glass handing it to them, before sitting on the other chair.

"A toast to new beginnings!"

The chink of glass signalled their approval, although they had not the first idea of just what new beginnings he had in mind...

# Nine

The room was silent, as Sagittarius sat there defiantly. It was not easy, as his body seemed to have a mind of its own.

"It is no use trying to resist, Professor."

The younger suited man looked at him, as he grimaced.

"We already know what you have been up to."

Sagittarius frowned, still gritting his teeth.

"It is a real pity, as you would have been very useful to us. We can always use an intelligent and creative man."

There was no way that he was going to let them use him, although with Taurus holding the gun, and the Doctor ready to administer another injection, it looked as though he was going to have great difficulty in stopping them!

"You were lucky last time, but your luck seems to have run out."

Despite what he thought, Sagittarius still clung onto hope, which, at this point in time seemed to be all that he did have!

"All of your research and your father's is now in our hands, and I must commend you for the way that you not only stole information from the Department, but in the way you used it. It was very ingenious, adapting your own nano robots to counter ours. Sadly for you, your efforts have been in vain, as there is now nothing that can stop us taking over."

Sagittarius had the feeling that it was not just the Department he was talking about...

"We now control the Secret Service here, and are working to control the secret services in many other countries too, not to mention the Government. It will not be long before we control everything."

It certainly looked as though it was indeed *checkmate*.

Back inside the wine bar, Oracle was still monitoring everything that was being said, and his scans confirmed that there were many traces of the foreign nano robots active within the SIS building. He also suspected that there were many others active outside, but the fly had a limited range, and what he really needed was to find a way of linking up with a more powerful device. It was then that he suddenly remembered the news bulletin, and in particular about the communications satellite that had been launched. If only he could tap into that, then he would be able to bounce a signal off it and get the information that he sought.

Whilst he was working out a way of doing that, the other Sagittarius was having a charm offensive, and the two young women, particularly after a few glasses of wine, were like *putty* in his hands. It seemed as though they had not a care in the world, both feeling happy and contented. That was in complete contrast to the barman, who whilst waiting for his next order was watching the television screen.

*We have some breaking news just in. The Government has just announced that it is taking the unprecedented step of closing all UK borders.*

It was the barman's turn to frown.

*Information is just reaching us that the 'Bat Flu' epidemic is now officially designated as a 'pandemic'. Government sources have admitted that the situation is very serious, and we are now going over to our Chief Political Correspondent.*

The picture changed, to show a man standing outside Downing Street.

*Yes, it looks as though things are very serious indeed, and it is not since the Second World War that the country has faced such a crisis.*

The picture changed to show the main news room.

*So, for the benefit of our viewers, can you tell us a little more about this 'Bat Flu'.*

The picture changed back to Downing Street.

*We are expecting a statement from the Prime Minister at any moment, but before he comes out, I will briefly run through what information we have.*

The barman looked glum. There were not going to be any foreign tourists for a while, which meant that there were not going to be as many tips. He relied upon them for his little luxuries, and if the borders were now going to be closed, then there were no longer going to be any imports, which meant no luxuries either!

*Well, we first heard about this about a month ago when someone was taken ill here in London. At first doctors were unsure of what exactly it was, and it was only after that person sadly died that they were able to do an autopsy. What they discovered, was that there was a virus which attacks the brain. It was something that they had never come in contact with before and, after further investigation, they discovered that it was a derivative of the Nipah virus, so called as it originally broke out in Nipah, Malaysia. Now, for those of you like me, who have never heard of it, it apparently enters the food chain via pigs.*

The barman went pale, wishing that he had not eaten that ham sandwich for his lunch!

*It is difficult to know exactly where it started, although it is suspected that imported meat from the Far East is the source. Normally it would just be a case of withdrawing all pork products from sale. However, once someone has contracted the disease, it is possible to pass the virus on via physical contact.*

The barman instinctively reached for the anti-bacterial spray.

*That could be by simply shaking hands with someone, or touching a surface which has already been touched by an infected person.*

The barman quickly sprayed the anti-bacterial spray on the surface of the bar.

*Now I don't have to tell you, how the news will be received by the general public, although the Government will be trying to allay fears.*

The anti-bacterial spray continued to flow as the correspondent's voice spread alarm.

*The Government insists that it has the situation under control, as it has a stockpile of vaccines already in place, with plans already drawn up to distribute them. However, for those unlucky enough to contract the virus, there is a 75% chance that they will not survive!*

The barman dropped the bottle of anti-bacterial spray, causing people to look round.

*The Opposition have already criticised the distribution plans, warning that they could cause panic and civil unrest. There have even been calls for the Army to be brought out onto the streets to assist the Police.*

It was all getting a bit much for the barman, who poured himself a stiff drink, knocking it back in one!

*I have just been told that the Prime Minister is about to emerge, so I will leave you with our cameraman and sound crew.*

With that, the picture changed, focussing on the large black door of 10 Downing Street, flanked by two armed police men. The door suddenly opened, and flash lights went off as the press eagerly took pictures of the Prime Minister walking calmly towards the waiting microphones.

*Good evening.*

The barman stopped what he was doing, muttering to himself.

"There's nothing good about it – bloomin' typical!"

*Today, unfortunately, I have to announce that we are in the grip of a 'pandemic', and as such I have had to take the appropriate action. All UK borders have now been closed until further notice, and all pork products have been recalled. We are embarking on a program of vaccination, and urge the public to remain calm. I have called an emergency COBRA meeting (Cabinet Office Briefing Room A) where we will be drawing up further plans, and a further statement will be made shortly, thank you.*

With that, the Prime Minister left to many questions from the waiting press.

58

Oracle had recorded every word, with a suspicion that everything was not quite as it seemed...


Back inside Interview Room One, the press conference had also been played on the computer, with the sound reverberating from the little speakers. The two suited men looked very pleased, in complete contrast to Sagittarius, who was still frowning.

"You see, Professor, now that we have all of the nano technology, it will only be a matter of time before those we have selected will be under our direct control, and as for the others..."

He struggled against the restraints, incensed at what he was hearing. But try as he might, there was no way that he was going to break the hold they had upon him.

"Now, now Professor, all resistance is futile!"

It certainly looked and felt like that, and as he stopped struggling, Sagittarius managed to get one of his own words out.

"Why?"

All four of the men smiled, content in the knowledge that everything was now working out according to *The Plan*.

"Being as you are not going to be here for very much longer, I think that it would be a good idea to tell you. Give you something to think about as the Doctor here ascertains just what those nano robots of yours have been up to."

Sagittarius looked towards doctor Crawley.

"We are in effect going to use you as a *guinea pig*."

The Doctor gave him a creepy look that did more to intimidate him than any gun waving by Taurus. He really was an odd looking man, thin and wiry with a sallow complexion, and greasy hair that fell in strands across his face.

"We intend to *cull* the ever increasing UK population down to a more *manageable* level. You see, being an island it will be an ideal test scenario. With the population at least halved, we will be able to directly control the survivors."

Sagittarius gave the younger suited man a horrified look.

"The *Bat Flu pandemic* is an ideal way of injecting people with our nano robots, and with you out of the equation, there will be no one to stop us!"

He tried to move again, pushing against his restraints, but there was still no way of shifting them.

"Once we have the UK under control, we will also have the world's financial system within our hands, after all the *City of London* is the financial hub of the planet."

It seemed as though they had thought of everything.

"When we have got that under our belts, we then intend to use the new private communications satellite network to go global…"

# Ten

The wine bar was deserted, apart from a few early evening drinkers mulling over the news, and wondering what fate had in store for them. Apart from a few hushed tones, most of the sound was coming from the television set, which was giving out further details as they emerged. No one actually knew what was going on, and even the newscaster, although trying to remain professional, showed signs of strain.

*We are still awaiting a Government statement, although we are receiving reports that the Army is readying itself and all reservists have been called up. All Police leave has been cancelled, and all medical personnel have been urged to report to their places of employment.*

"Bloomin marvellous!"

The barman sprayed the anti-bacterial spray on the already disinfected surface of the bar, as his glum mood spread like the proverbial *black cloud.*

*We also understand that there will be a call for everyone to return to their homes and await the Government statement, although few people are heeding this, as we have other reports of panic buying, as people stock up on supplies.*

The barman poured himself another drink, looking over towards the three people huddled around a table by the window. They seemed oblivious to the situation, and the two very attractive young women were so wrapped up in the smartly dressed man that the news meant nothing to them. The barman was single, and as he drank from his glass, he wondered just what the man's secret was. He did have a secret, although it was one which the barman would never be able to guess!

The other Sagittarius was busily *reeling* the young women into his own plan, like a fisherman, who after dangling the bait, was now ready with his big net to land his *catch*. Their fixation with him grew as he promised them many things, although the only thing they really wanted was him!

Oracle sat in disgust in his Gladstone bag. The real Sagittarius would never have acted in such a way, and even though he was a *cyber rabbit*, he had morals and scruples gained from his creator. He was toying with the idea of emerging from his bag, and sinking his front teeth into his leg, injecting him with a large dose of his own nano robots. Oracle knew, however, that he had to be patient, as more information was flooding into his processor all of the time.

Everything that had been going on in the room where the real Sagittarius was being held had been received via the fly, and the transmitter embedded in his fob watch. It confirmed his suspicions, and he was busily making plans of his own.

*Breaking news!*

The television blurted out its warning, and the barman took another drink from his rapidly emptying glass.

*We now have the Government statement, which is as follows:*

*Britain is facing one of its sternest tests, and the appropriate action is being taken. All military, police and medical personnel are to report to their allotted places of employment. All civilians are to return to their homes and stay there until further notice. 'Martial Law' will be declared from midnight tonight, and looters will be dealt with in the strongest terms.*

62

*Supplies of the vaccine are being distributed to Hospitals and Medical Centres, and lists are being drawn up of those to be inoculated. This will be done via National Insurance numbers, which will be published via the internet and local media. When your number is called, you will proceed to your nearest medical centre, hospital, or makeshift centres which are being opened in schools and community centres. Identification is required, and anyone who fails to provide adequate identification will be arrested and held in makeshift detention centres.*

The barman emptied his glass.

"Bloomin' heck!"

It certainly sounded as though draconian measures were now in place, and as he watched the report, he began to wonder if the bar should close. He was not the only one, as the bar manager suddenly appeared.

"I think that it is best if we close up soon."

The barman looked worried. Not only had he missed out on a few tips, but he also faced the prospect of being laid off. He doubted whether they would continue paying him, as he was on a zero hours contract. His wages were not very generous, and he now had not only the worry of the *Bat Flu pandemic*, but also of how he was going to pay his bills. London was certainly not a cheap place to live, and he was not only facing a medical crisis, but a financial one too!

Whilst the manager was talking to the barman, there was the bleep of a mobile phone. It was in the pocket of the other Sagittarius, who calmly reached into his jacket, pulling it out.

There was a text message, and it was quite simple, *Return to HQ*. Head Quarters was back in the SIS building, and a look of disappointment filled his face. He had planned to go to *Lamborn Road* and enjoy the comforts of not only the real Sagittarius's home, but also of the two young women whom he had so carefully been plying with alcohol.

Oracle twitched his whiskers, almost smiling to himself. Smiling was one thing which a cyber rabbit could not do, but if it could then he would have had a big grin from ear to ear!

"Duty calls!"

He spoke with a resigned tone.

"I'm afraid that I have been ordered back to HQ!"

A look of disappointment also filled their faces, as they were enjoying themselves.

"What about us?"

Gemini suddenly realised that they had nowhere to go. They only had what was with them, and being as they had handed over the credit card earlier, they had no money either!

They both felt helpless, as they sat there stunned.

"Don't worry, you are coming with me. I couldn't just abandon you."

A very relieved look greeted his statement, as they both took a sip of wine before each kissing him on a cheek.

"Thank you!"

They both spoke at the same time, staring adoringly into his eyes.

Oracle could see what was going on through the fabric of his bag, and if he could have been able to give a look of disgust, then he would. Having neutralised the foreign nano robots within their bodies, he had also removed most of their personalities. Now he realised that he would have to do something to give them some independence. They were so vulnerable, and whilst he had thought that it would be better to let the real Sagittarius guide their recovery, now that he had been replaced by the *doppelgänger*, Oracle would have to take matters into his own hands.

What he really needed was a squad of *stealth rabbits*, after all he had to rescue the real Sagittarius from deep inside the SIS building. Once he did that, they would then have to try to neutralise the foreign nano robots within the building, and then set to work on trying to deal with the *Bat Flu pandemic*. It looked as though he needed a miracle!

There was only one person that he could call however, and that was Big Jim.


More than a hundred miles away, Big Jim was sitting at his computer trying to get some more information about the pandemic, having, like most people, heard the Government announcement.

Things looked grim, and having had first hand experience of the vaccine, he knew what it really contained. To him, it looked as though the whole thing was nothing more than a *smoke screen* for the Organisation to take over the whole country. If that was not worrying enough, he feared that they would release the real virus after they had inoculated all those they wished to save!

It was *genocide*, and a deliberate attempt to not only control the populace, but also to *cull* all those they thought were not going to be of any use to them. It was a truly dreadful situation, and one which he knew he had to do something about.

When Oracle's message flashed up on his screen, he looked horrified.

*Department compromised.*

*Sagittarius held prisoner in the SIS building.*

*Gemini and Caprica at risk.*

*Assistance required!!!*

He sat stroking his beard, wondering what he could do. How could one man and a *cyber rabbit* take on the might of the Organisation?

# Eleven

The sun began to set, giving off an unnatural red glow that filled the sky, as if the whole world was bleeding. They always said that *red sky at night was the shepherds delight*, but sadly not on this occasion. Tomorrow's weather would start off fine, but before too long, it would change, as there was a storm brewing.

The change would not only be in the weather, for in the morning, vaccinations would start, and everything would change. Gone would be the democracy that so many had fought to maintain over the years. Big Jim thought of his father, struggling to crack the Enigma code. That was deemed to be impossible, and yet the brains of the nation had managed to do it, thus shortening the course of the Second World War by up to two years.

There was not a code that could not be broken, nor anything that was totally secure. Now, he would have to work through the night, using every bit of his knowledge and experience to try and break into the Organisation's systems.

That task was just as difficult as finding out just who they were, and where they were based. It appeared that the Organisation was global, and there were only a few people that he could contact. They were mostly retired, and outside the proverbial loop.

He could try, although most of them already thought that he was living in the *realms of fantasy* as it was!

The whole thing seemed so far fetched that he even had doubts about it himself. Who would believe that there was a group of people trying to take over the world?

He sat stroking his beard, wondering where to start.

The message from Oracle seemed dire, as his son and the two young women who had accompanied him to London were in great danger, and sitting here he could not really do anything to help them. There were a few *blessings* though, as he did have a direct link to Oracle's processor. He got the details up on his screen, and initially Oracle seemed to be working well. However, when he looked at them a little closer, he found that there were a few anomalies.

For a start, being just a *machine,* Oracle should work on pure logic, either a thing *is* or it is *not*. Everything should come down to *Binary Logic*, where things should either be *black* or *white*. It was as though he was now using a wider range of concepts to come to a conclusion. He was somehow becoming almost *human*, as he had an understanding that there was more to a *thing* than the sum of its *parts*, and also understood the relationship of the *parts* when combined into a *whole*.

It was as though Oracle was developing certain traits, which he would not have expected a *cyber rabbit* to have. For a start, he was beginning to take on some human emotions, which was something quite unexpected. Maybe it was something to do with the foreign nano robots, that had in some way contaminated him, or maybe he was growing in experience?

It was extraordinary to think that a *cyber rabbit* could experience emotions, and somehow he was learning not only what they were, but also how to use them!

Big Jim's diagnostic program split Oracle's behavioural trends into certain groupings, and as he studied them, he began to realise that Oracle was exhibiting traits he would associate with some of the five natural emotions, love, fear, anger, envy and grief.

From what Big Jim could see, it was mostly based around love, which he liked to think was the only true emotion. In Big Jim's mind, everything was an expression of love, and when given and received unconditionally, it brought joy and happiness, spreading kindness, compassion and affection. When it was repressed or became difficult to express, it lead to *fear*. To him, the Organisation was spreading fear, and perceived everyone outside it as a threat.

For some reason Oracle had no fear, and wanted not just to protect his son, but also to make him happy. He did not appear to experience anger either, just a practical ability to neutralise any perceived danger. He would first analyse a situation, and then act accordingly. Oracle seemed to have a perception of things, and used his sensors of sight and hearing to make decisions.

He had only been what he termed *fully operational* for a matter of months, following his latest upgrade, although he had been in development for years. Every upgrade increased his capabilities, and he had a hand in what his son had been trying to achieve. Oracle was mostly Sagittarius's work, and the two shared a symbiotic existence, as all of Sagittarius's memories had been downloaded into Oracle's processor. They both thought and acted in the same way, although there was definitely a marked difference developing between them.

Oracle had begun to exhibit certain qualities that the other cyber rabbits or *lads*, as he liked to call them, did not have. It was as though in some ways he was becoming *sentient*.

When he began to analyse his behaviour, Big Jim noticed that Oracle was developing a *mischievous* side to his nature, and had begun to do things which deviated from his original programming. It was difficult to put his finger on just what it was, but there was certainly something. He could sense that Sagittarius was uncomfortable around women, and that was something which he seemed to be taking quite an interest in!

The more uncomfortable his son became, the more Oracle played on the situation. Having wiped Gemini and Caprica's memories when ridding them of the foreign nano robots, it was as though he was trying to *matchmake*. Organic rabbits have a reputation for procreation, and it was as though he desired to experience that side of his nature via Sagittarius.

The whole scenario was just as complicated as that of the Organisation, and the more that Big Jim thought about it, the more he came to the same conclusion. Oracle was becoming a little *too* independent for his liking!

The fundamental reason for his existence was to assist his son, and to carry information which he shared via the neuron interface of both the nano robots and the dark glasses. He was originally created to resemble a childhood pet, and also carried several defensive capabilities. Big Jim had expected Oracle to do something, instead of just sitting in his Gladstone bag, although when he thought more about that, there was not much that he could have done. Maybe it was a good thing that he had remained *undercover?*

If Oracle had become *sentient*, then that would be a giant leap forward, and if that was discovered, then heaven knows what the Organisation would do if they got their hands on such technology!

Still pondering, he began to delve a little deeper into what Oracle had been working on, and was quite shocked at what he discovered.

Big Jim had dedicated many years of his life to trying to help those with nerve damage, and others who struggled with artificial limbs. His dream had been to enable the brain to reconnect with those parts of the body that would no longer respond to its commands, and to also control artificial limbs. Much of his research had been downloaded into Oracle's processor, and he was staggered at just what Oracle had done with it.

The human body basically consists of a collection of molecules, and although most of it is water, it also contains many chemicals. There are traces of metals, such as *zinc, magnesium,* and *potassium,* and these combine to form an electric current. Although this current is very small, it can be detected.

Brain cells communicate by sending tiny electric signals to each other, and the more signals that are sent, the more electricity the brain will produce. Big Jim had used an *EEG* (electroencephalogram) to measure the pattern of this electrical activity, and discovered that active areas of the brain use more energy than less active parts. His research had also led to what was termed *PET* (Positron Emission Tomography) and *FMRI* (Functional Magnetic Resonance Imaging) or Functional Scanning. It was very sophisticated technology, and during his years of research he had discovered that not only does the human brain generate electricity, but also the body does. The blood flowing through the veins and arteries has metallic traces, and just like a magnet, it has its own *magnetic field.*

71

Big Jim stroked his beard as he sat there with a mixture of disbelief and elation. His research had also led him into other ways of detecting the magnetic field of the body, such as the use of a *Kirlian camera.*

In 1939 Semyon Kirlian discovered how to capture the electrical field, or *aura* surrounding living things using photography. To create these images, he sent an electric current through an object and captured the aura image on a photographic plate.

What Oracle had discovered was that the foreign nano robots affected the body's natural aura. At the very top of the aura, there is what looks like a fountain of light, and its seven *petals* resemble a *flowering lotus.*

The aura itself comprises of the seven colours of the rainbow, although the *colour* is actually the frequency of that wave, as each colour has a different wavelength.

The *halo* is normally either a *bluish* or *yellowish* colour, and if a person has dubious thoughts, or has told a lie, then greenish yellow shoots appears through the halo, combined with a muddy brown. In those being controlled by the foreign nano robots, the *halo* appeared to be brown, with just one strong green shoot in the middle.

By switching his visual receptors to resemble a *Kirlian Camera*, Oracle could now instantly see who had been infected.

It was a real break though, and as he switched his screen back towards the data being transmitted he had an idea. Why not configure any visual information to resemble a *Kirlian Camera*, then he could see for himself?

It only took him a few minutes to make the necessary changes, and when he had, he linked it directly to the *fly*.

The fly appeared to be working well, and Big Jim was receiving an audio signal that was surprisingly clear considering the circumstances. The visual signal kept on breaking up though, but it was just good enough to show him that his son was held in a chair by some rather tough looking restraints. The picture also showed that everyone in the room was being controlled by the foreign nano robots, including the two suited men sitting behind the desk.

He had assumed that they were the *ring leaders*, although there were undoubtedly others above them, as the Organisation seemed to have many levels.

He could also see the revolver hovering over his son's head, and remembered how Taurus had shot him without a blink of his eye. He seemed totally ruthless, as did the men sitting behind the desk. The doctor also seemed very sinister, and the whole scenario made him feel sick!

The fly was transmitting information, and the more that he heard, the less he liked. It seemed as though they were dealing with a group of fanatics willing to sacrifice millions of people in order to get what they wanted - total control!

People were not truly free as it was, condemned to a life of work to pay the bills. They had to live somewhere and have food, water and all of the other basic necessities of life. For those who could not find work, or who were not fit to work, it seemed as though the struggle to survive was even harder. Rich politicians had some big ideas, all of which in his opinion seemed to make things even worse. Their lives were a lot easier as they had the wealth and contacts to make sure that they were protected from the hardships most people faced.

Big Jim was not a fan of politicians, although every now and then there seemed to be one or two who tried to do their best. Sadly, they were soon either discredited or sidelined, as the system rolled on like one large conveyor belt. It was all *secret committees* and *old school ties*, and even the communist system had proved that corruption was so rife that conditions for normal people never really improved. Now it was going to get a whole lot worse, and he had to do something about it!

The fly was receiving quite a broad spectrum of signals from the room, and they were being transmitted on several wavebands. He already knew which ones the foreign nano robots used, but there were also some new ones, which he found puzzling to understand.

There was no doubt a similar *bug* within the room, recording and transmitting data which could account for some of them, and possibly one which, if he could isolate it, would release the restraints on the chair. There was however, another much stronger signal, the type of which he had never seen before.

In some ways it was like a microwave, although he could not imagine anyone cooking themselves a quick snack under these conditions. There was another one which he recognised as the wave band used by mobile telephones.

Naturally, being the centre of the Secret Intelligence Service, there would be a whole host of things going on, but the largest signal seemed to be being transmitted from outside.

He closed this particular window down, and opened another, acting on a hunch. Within a few minutes, his hunch was confirmed, as he was picking up the signal, constantly being broadcast from a satellite.

Fortunately, Big Jim had a lot of programming experience, and although his hands were quite large, and his fingers not as nimble as they used to be, he was able to adapt some of his existing software to bring up a schematic of the Earth, showing where the signal was originating from.

The Earth looked a little like a tennis ball, with something rolling around it in a fixed orbit. He continued to improve his program, and noticed that there were several others, all transmitting the same signal, forming a type of *grid* that seemed to be focused almost entirely on the British isles. Each satellite swept in a low orbit, passing over the country before moving away. Then, another one would follow in a constant pattern, so that there was hardly a break. He also noticed, that the signal seemed to be switched off when the satellite got out of range, as the other one took over. Looking more closely, he suddenly realised that if whoever was controlling them really wanted too, then virtually the whole planet could be covered!

The news reports had confirmed that there was a new privately funded communications satellite system in operation, although they had not mentioned just what sort of communication it was transmitting. The signal worked on the same wavelength as the foreign nano robots and, as he studied what he was seeing, he came to a conclusion.

The satellites were now controlling the nano robots, and anyone who had them in their system would be linked to the *grid!*

It was like some weird futuristic film, where human robots were being controlled by a single terminal. Big Jim shuddered

75

at the thought. It was bad enough living in the most watched society on earth, with close circuit television recording virtually everything everyone did. That was another reason for moving to the country, where there was still some freedom. It looked as though freedom was going to be a thing of the past, particularly as everyone was going to be injected. Those unfortunate enough not to be selected, were going to be eliminated!

Big Jim just sat there as the enormity of the situation began to sink in. He had to try and jam that signal, as well as rescue his son, and by the looks of things, time was rapidly running out!

For a long time he had suspected that there was far more to the *secret societies* and groups of rich industrialists than most people realised. For a start, they seemed to control most things, and had influence over not just business, but governments too. It seemed as though there was another tier above those who were supposed to be in charge, who had the ability to *pull the strings* from behind the scene. It was a murky, undercover world, and one which he had encountered before.

On his last contract, when he had discovered that his research was going to be used to control people instead of helping them, it had shocked him. It was a far cry from the *halcyon days* of youth, when his generation set out to change the world. *Love and peace* had been their goals, but sadly there seemed to be little of that today. People had turned to *greed* and *power*, with workplace bullying, shareholders' profits and avariciousness being the norm. Just how much money did anyone really need?

There was a level of comfort, which when attained, there seemed to be no logic in surpassing. Long gone were the *philanthropists* who sunk their money into social welfare and improving the conditions of those they employed. What use

76

was amassing all of that money if you were not going to do anything worthwhile with it?

Big Jim was an idealist, and his beliefs seemed to be at odds with society. Once he found out about what they had planned to do with his research, he had left, but not before doing a little investigation.

What he discovered was that big decisions were taken in secret, at prearranged meetings in luxury hotels or *gentleman's clubs*. The stock market was manipulated, and even those few courageous individuals who stood defiantly against what was planned seemed to disappear in one way or another. They had *unfortunate* accidents, or were the victims of *assassination*. It certainly was a dangerous and frightening world. He was glad that he had got out when he did, although judging by what had happened only days before, he was caught up in all again. Now, it seemed as though it was up to him to help his son in overcoming the latest and most serious situation to affect the unsuspecting public.

It was going to be virtually impossible to get to those in charge, but the one thing that he could do was to temporarily thwart their plans.

What was needed was to create a computer virus, one which could disrupt the transmission.

Big Jim sighed, stroking his beard.

It would take time to create, and even his programming skills would be pushed to the limit. That was not the only problem though, as even if he did manage to create one, he still did not have the delivery system to upload it!

Thinking hard, he suddenly had an idea. There was someone who did, and that someone was GCHQ (Government Communications Headquarters) in Cheltenham. So, all he need now, was to somehow get inside!

Back inside the room, Sagittarius was still trying to resist the foreign nano robots, as well as trying to understand just how people who obviously came from a privileged background could act in such a way. It just seemed so *alien* to him, and in many ways he was quite like his father. However, it was no use thinking of how life should be, what he really needed to do was to focus his thoughts on breaking free, then perhaps he could do something to stop them!

"It is useless to struggle, Professor."

The words broke his *train of thought*, having a self confidence tinged with more than a little arrogance. The younger suited man was watching him wriggle, as the restraints clasping both his arms and legs seemed to almost weld him to the chair.

He looked into the suited man's eyes.

"Why?"

"Why, Professor because we can!"

Sagittarius was playing for time, keeping him talking whilst he hoped that somehow he could break free. That was the least of his problems, as the revolver was still hovering, menacingly, pointed towards his head.

"We are so grateful to you, Professor. You have not been the only one to do research into nano technology, and now that we have perfected it, thanks to your research I may add, we have the means to do what we always wished to do."

He was trying to make Sagittarius feel guilty, to blame himself for what was about to happen. It was a classic case of *passing the buck,* and of the sort of mind games people within the Organisation liked to play.

"The public does not really know what is good for them, and in fighting us, you have missed a glorious opportunity."

It did not sound that glorious to him!

"A certain pattern imprinted on the neuron cortex can produce a mental or physical reaction, but you already know this!"

He was talking about what effect the nano robots had on the human brain.

"The entire spectrum of human emotions can now be affected, avoiding the use of a host of drugs such as tranquillizers, ending such things as depression. At the touch of a button anything from sleep to euphoria, can instantly be transmitted."

Sagittarius knew that the pharmaceutical industry would not like that for a moment and, being so powerful, they were undoubtedly involved in this in one way or another. After all, who else would have the mass production capabilities?

To hear him speak it was as though he was doing a great service to the nation, offering miracle cures, but the one thing that he did not mention was *freedom!*

"You yourself have experienced what healing powers nano technology can provide."

On this occasion he was correct, although his gun shot wound would not have needed healing if he had not been shot by Taurus in the first place!

"Not all people are equal, and some are born to lead, whilst others are born to follow."

It seemed as though the f*eudal* system was back with a vengeance, even though with the *old school tie brigade* it had never really left!

"When we have over population, what better way to rid ourselves of that drain on resources."

Sagittarius had studied body language and behavioural patterns whilst constructing Oracle. Here was clearly someone so delusional that he actually believed they were doing good, when in fact, they were embarking on nothing short of mind control and *genocide!*

The other suited figure had been nodding along with everything his colleague had been saying, and between them they represented everything that he had fought against all his life. Now he needed some help, and his thoughts turned to his trusted friend and companion Oracle…

# Twelve

A rather elegantly dressed man in his early fifties, wearing a smartly tailored black suit, adjusted his glasses as he finished speaking to the barman. The manager, a man of over twenty five years experience in the licensed trade, was unaccustomed to closing early. To him there seemed little choice, however he was concerned about getting home to *suburbia*.

His greying hair was testament to not only his age, but also the long unsociable hours he worked. Yes, he was able to delegate to his assistant manager, but the overall responsibility rested on his shoulders. The company who owned the wine bar, and in fact a whole chain of them, always seemed to be striving for ever increasing profit margins. It was a very good business, and made a considerable amount of money, but that never seemed to be enough for them. Walking from his office, having received the news about the current situation, he began to think the same thoughts that he had been having over the past few years. Maybe it was time to try and find somewhere else to work, which had shorter and more sociable hours?

He did not see enough of his family, and the travelling was also getting him down. Now, it looked as though there was a possibility of contracting this terrible disease, and the prospect of losing one, if not more of them.

He was not the only one in need of a stiff drink!

The manager calmly walked from behind the bar towards the first of his customers, and in a polite manner informed them that due to the present set of circumstances they would be closing, and he would be grateful if they would finish off their drinks.

Whilst he was doing that, the barman started to drape the towels over the beer pumps, signalling that the bar was indeed closing. He was still in a state of shock and wished that he could stay here, rather than trying to venture home. Unfortunately that was not a viable prospect, for the premises had no accommodation, as the upstairs had been turned into a restaurant.

He was still transfixed by the television, which was still blurting out information. It seemed that whenever there was something serious to report, the news team greeted it with a great deal of excitement, building whatever it was up from a dilemma into a crisis. On this occasion however, events did not need any stimuli. Things were very serious, and by the looks of it could soon be getting considerably worse!

*If you have just joined us, then here is an update on the current situation.*

The barman listened, taking little notice of the leaving customers.

*The 'Bat Flu' epidemic has now been classified as a 'Pandemic'.*

*All pork products have been withdrawn from supermarket shelves, and the public is advised not to eat pork, bacon or ham.*

*Columns of armed troops have begun to leave their barracks, as preparations are made for the imposition of a curfew which is due to start at midnight.*

*The public is urged to stay at home, unless their National Insurance numbers are selected. Numbers will be displayed on the bottom of the screen later, and be published on the internet.*

*Makeshift vaccination centres are being set up in schools and community centres, as well as hospital and medical centres.*

*We also have reports of panic buying, and some civil unrest, although it is currently nowhere near as large or widespread as first feared.*

"Bloomin' wonderful!"

The barman hoped that he could avoid trouble on his way home, and that public transport would still be running. He was still *glued* to the screen as the manager worked his way around the remainder of the people left in the bar before finally stopping at the table by the window.

The other Sagittarius and his two, slightly merry companions informed him that they were already in the process of leaving, much to his relief. He would have to cancel all restaurant bookings as well as send the chef and the other catering staff home early. If he was lucky, then he might just make it home himself before the curfew!

Oracle could sense the multiple emotions within the wine bar, fear, uncertainty, apprehension and disappointment - the latter, coming from the other Sagittarius. He had big plans for this evening, and was hoping that his recall was just going to be a temporary set back. However, little did he realise just was plans had been made for him!

Oracle had plans of his own and, as they finished off their drinks, he was busily making last minute adjustments to what he was about to do...

# Thirteen

The sound of a siren pierced the air as they stood by the door waiting to leave, its harsh tones reverberating in their ears as a police car rushed past with its blue lights flashing. It was probably answering a *999* telephone call, which did little to allay the fears of the barman. He looked over, wondering if any trouble had broken out.

The two young women seemed oblivious to it, as the other Sagittarius held the door open for them. It was nothing more than a large clear glass panel with a steel handle on either side, and opaque lettering engraved upon it bearing the name of the wine bar:

INTRIGUE.

It certainly seemed appropriate, and yet another one of Sagittarius's coincidences. Unfortunately, he was not here to appreciate it, as he was still being held in the SIS building. His *doppelgänger* had taken over his identity, waiting for the two very attractive young women to venture out on to the pavement, after plying them with alcohol.

The air was still quite warm, in contrast to the air conditioning of the wine bar, and as it hit them, its effect made them titter. The other Sagittarius cursed his luck, wishing that he had taken them straight to a hotel room, but it was too late now, and he hoped that it would not take long in the SIS building. Plastic surgery may have altered his outward appearance, but he was really far less of the gentleman than the real Sagittarius had always been!

His task was to impersonate the Head of Experimental Department and pass on as much information as he could.

Now, with his mission almost completed, he was not sure what the Organisation had planned for him?

Oracle was being carried in his Gladstone bag, all part of the deception, and could see what was going on through the fabric that encased him. He had decided to give the two young women an upgrade via the friendly nano robots within their bodies. They would have to play a part in what he had in mind, although by the look of them, they had enough trouble in walking let alone doing anything else!

The evening had a strange calm about it, with only a few people in the usually busy streets. They were mostly employees rushing to get home before the curfew started. Some of them were wearing face masks, whilst others held handkerchiefs to their noses, clearly worried about being infected. Little did they realise that infection would take place when they were inoculated, and the whole scenario was nothing more than the most devious plan the *Organisation* had ever embarked upon.

An empty bus trundled past on its way back to the depot, as the late evening sunshine shone off its traditional red paintwork. A black taxi cab followed on behind crammed full of people, even though the driver had doubled his fares to take advantage of the situation. All of those desperate people trying to get home had made it very profitable, and after he dropped them off, he too was heading home.

All went quiet for a few moments, until the sound of vehicles made them look round. In the distance they could just make out an armoured column moving slowly towards the SIS building. If they were quick, then they would just make it before the column arrived.

85

Gemini tottered and giggled on her heels, as Caprica clung to her, also giggling. They were not taking the slightest bit of notice of the *pandemic*, as they thought that they had finally got their man, and nothing else seemed to matter.

The other Sagittarius helped them across the road, and just as they approached the gatehouse, the convoy drew to a halt.

"Back again so soon Professor?"

The security man smiled at his exasperated expression. Both young women had trouble walking, and as the smell of alcohol wafted over him, he could only imagine what they would have been up to if he had not been recalled due to the crisis. Waving them through he sighed, wondering where he had gone wrong?

It was just as easy to get into the main building, as the other security guard said, and thought the exact same thing. It was the first time that either of them had ever seen the Professor accompanied by a women, and today he had two very attractive ones, if slightly the worse for wear!

The other Sagittarius left them in reception, along with Oracle, as he registered at the main desk. They sat down on the comfortable seats, giggling again like a pair of *schoolgirls*, much to the disdain of the receptionist!

Once signed in, he gave them a cheery wave, which was reciprocated as he moved towards the lift. Once the button had been pressed, it only took a few moments for the door to open, and they watched him disappear inside.

This was Oracle's chance, and before they knew what had hit them, he transmitted his prepared data. They instantly felt something change within them, and the signals transformed them from a couple of giggly *schoolgirls,* into what could only be described as a pair of *zombies!*

All emotion instantly drained from their faces, as they sat back closing their eyes, just as if they were asleep. They may have seemed calm and tranquil on the outside, but on the inside it was something completely different. Oracle had worked out just what they needed to do to execute his plan, and he was hoping that he would have enough time before they executed the real Sagittarius!

The lift pinged, indicating that it had reached the designated floor, and the doors duly opened, allowing the other Sagittarius to exit. He was curious as to why they had sent for him, thinking that he had completed his mission. Working for the Organisation, however, meant that just like *Shakespeare's Shylock*, they demanded their full *pound of flesh.*

The Personal Assistant was expecting him and quickly showed him through into the main room, where he was greeted by the others.

"Welcome back, Mr Sagittarius."

The younger suited man's tone was less than welcoming and it was clear that he had an ulterior motive.

"We have another little task for you to perform."

That was the signal for the Doctor to briefly leave the room, and the younger suited man smirked as he walked past him.

Sagittarius wondered what was going on, just like his counterpart, and they were not left wondering for long, because the Doctor soon returned, pushing a piece of electronic equipment on a trolley.

87

It seemed to comprise of a lot of wires connected to a central console, looking a little like a mixing desk with lots of knobs and buttons. He moved it past the desk, bringing it to rest next to the Professor. The Doctor then left, returning with another chair, which he placed at the other side of the apparatus.

"Would you care to sit, Mr Sagittarius."

This was not a request, more a demand, and knowing just how they operated, he did as he was instructed. The Doctor then plugged the apparatus into the mains socket, and several lights began to flash, and dials move as it powered up. He then placed an electrode on either temple, before turning towards Sagittarius.

"Now it is your turn, Professor!"

That sounded ominous, with the younger suited man giving him a smirk, as the Doctor reached over towards him. He shook his head in protest, but Taurus moved closer, pointing his revolver to the side of his face. So, reluctantly, Sagittarius allowed the Doctor to place an electrode on each of his temples too.

"We are now going to transfer all of your memories Professor, so that Mr Sagittarius here can benefit from not only all that you have ever done, but also everything that you have ever thought of doing."

Sagittarius looked horrified. If they succeeded, then they would know all about Oracle and, whatever happened, he could not allow that. With their resources it would only be a matter of time before they constructed their own *cyber rabbits!*

"Just think, in only a matter of minutes the transformation will be complete, and then we will no longer need you. Everyone will assume that Mr Sagittarius is actually you - not that they do not think that already."

Sagittarius frowned.

"We in the Organisation have some very creative ways of dealing with unwanted people."

It was Taurus's turn to smirk. He got a real thrill out of that sort of thing, and the foreign nano robots inside his body had turned him into a bit of a *monster*.

"When you are ready, Doctor."

It looked as though there was no way of stopping them and, even though he struggled against the restraints, he just could not break free...

# Fourteen

A melodious hum pulsed from the apparatus, and more lights flashed, as the dials swung from side to side, before the signal began to stabilise. At first there was no sensation, then as the power continued to build up, both men felt a tingling sensation, making their scalps itch as the electrical current forced its way through the protective layer of bone into their brains.

Unbeknown to everyone, apart that was from Sagittarius, the fly was still positioned on the wall above his head, and its transmission had constantly been sent to Oracle. Just like a man with his head in the *guillotine*, he had been waiting for a reprieve, which looked as though it was not going to arrive.

Everything suddenly went dark, and he presumed that it was the electrodes, firing electric impulses into his brain. He could also hear noises, which again he thought were a side effect of whatever they were doing to him. Nothing in fact, could have been further from the truth!

Just like the proverbial *Cavalry*, Oracle had arrived in the *nick of time*. He was now out of his Gladstone bag, and had hacked into the buildings power supply, killing everything on this floor.

In the confusion, he had managed to taser Taurus and the Doctor, and as soon as the lights came back on again, there standing holding taser guns were Gemini and Caprica.

Sagittarius could not believe what he was seeing, thinking that it was his mind playing tricks on him. It was no illusion however, as they were very real, and by the look on their faces, they were very determined too!

They may have been wearing flimsy little summer dresses, but by the way they were holding their guns, they looked as though they were a lot tougher than their clothing suggested.

"Don't anyone move!"

Gemini barked out her order in a strong commanding tone, as the two suited men looked at her with very worried expressions on their faces. The tables had now been turned and, by the look of them, they did not like it at all!

Oracle was also in no mood to compromise, and sunk his teeth into Taurus's backside, making him wince as he struggled to cope with the effect of the taser pulse. The Doctor also felt a similar sensation, and the nano robots injected into their blood streams quickly took effect, sending them in to a comatose state.

The other Sagittarius did not move, wondering what he was going to do, until he too felt the sharp pain of Oracle's front teeth digging into the back of his ankle.

It now only left the two suited men, whose discomfort grew as the restrains holding Sagittarius suddenly sprang open. He wasted not time in getting up, pulling the electrodes off his temples, with a rush of blood flooding through his veins. Just like in his first encounter with the Doctor and his accomplices, he was ready for a fight!

Moving swiftly across the room, he grabbed hold of the younger suited man by the neck, pulling him to his feet as his free hand drew back ready to punch. The man went white, with all of his bravado evaporating as he waited to feel the full force of Sagittarius's temper.

The other man, who had remained silent, just sat there impassively as he had done throughout the interrogation. He was certainly a cool customer, and obviously the real one in charge.

Sagittarius felt a hand on his arm, and as he looked round he saw the Personal Assistant standing there shaking her head.

"Special Agent Bond, Jayne Bond, I'm on your side."

He was dumbfounded, the whole situation seemed unreal. Not only had he come very close to having his entire memory transferred to his *doppelgänger,* and then face a very untimely end, now there was a *Special Agent* who went by the name of *Bond.* Things had gone from the *sublime* to the *ridiculous,* and he half expected her to follow that with *007!*

"Bond?"

"Yes, S.I.G. (Special Intelligence Group)"

Sagittarius had heard rumours of such a unit, a very secretive top level one, although he, like most people even within the Security Service, did not know for sure whether it existed or not.

"We have been tracking the Organisation for quite some time, and were about to approach you when they got to you first."

That was cold comfort, as he had been injected with foreign nano robots twice, shot, and abducted again, not to mention all that had gone on at *Freedom Farm.*

"I have been working undercover, and read the report the agent made when he visited your parents' home."

Sagittarius felt a slight feeling of relief, at least there was someone on his side!

"There is not much time to talk right now."

He still did not know whether or not to trust her. The Organisation was very devious, and he would not put it past them to have a double agent at work. She was indeed a *double agent*, but apparently working on his side!

Sagittarius was still not sure, as she had appeared to be completely devoid of any emotions when she had been playing the mind games with him earlier.

"I know that you must have your doubts, but you can trust me."

Oracle ran a quick scan, and the results proved that she was *clean*. She could however, still be a part of the Organisation.

"Look, it is hard to explain!"

Sagittarius was going to take some convincing, and even if she was telling the truth, he still wanted to punch the younger suited man.

"We need him in one piece to gather intelligence."

That did make sense, although his desire to smash him into little pieces remained.

Whilst he deliberated, both suited men removed small oval capsules covered in brown rubber with their tongues, which had been attached to the back of their upper sets of teeth. Biting into the thin walled glass ampoule, they released deadly doses of *potassium cyanide*, which within seconds would cause brain death and heart failure.

There was nothing that could be done to stop them, and before anyone realised what was going on, both men had slumped in their seats.

"Damn!"

Special agent Bond cursed.

"Cyanide capsules!"

Sagittarius lowered his fist, as she quickly moved to examine them. They were both dead!

She wanted to take them alive, but they had taken the capsules to hide their knowledge of the Organisation before she had the chance to interrogate them.

"Cyanide?"

He could not believe it, it all sounded very far-fetched to him.

"Yes!"

Special Agent Bond left them, as there was nothing else that she could do.

"The Organisation is ruthless, even with itself. They reward success, and punish failure."

Sagittarius shivered at the thought.

They still had the Doctor and Taurus, who were certainly not the types to take their own lives. There was also the other Sagittarius, who sat there impassively. He was equally as concerned about his own life too, and being as they had all been recruited instead of being members of the Organisation, it made a real difference.

It looked as though there was going to be a lot of explaining to do, and in view of the seriousness of the situation, very little time to do it in!

Special Agent Bond pulled some plastic strips out of her suit pocked, handing them to him.

"Put these on them, whilst I cover you."

He did as he was asked, and within a few moments they were all bound by the hands and feet, much to his relief.

"Now, we must secure the building."

To Sagittarius's knowledge the whole building had been compromised, and he wondered how the four of them were going to liberate it.

"We have taken your supply of *stealth wasps* from your laboratory, along with certain other items. You will find them on floor two, room number 205. Here is the key."

She handed him a thin plastic strip.

"You must program and release them, and then get to GCHQ. They are using the transmitters to control the nano robots."

Government Communications Head Quarters, was where they provided signal intelligence, monitoring communications on a world wide basis. Sagittarius did not realise that they also had the ability to transmit signals too. It was all getting a bit too *cloak and dagger* for him. Sagittarius was basically just a scientist, and was driven by his desire to create Oracle. He had never thought for one moment that he would end up becoming what amounted to a *007!*

To him, it had all been a story, just like so many other people who had seen the films. Now he was literally going to have to *act* his *part*, although this was far more than fiction. What had happened to him so far was very real, a little too real when he came to think about it!

It was as though there was a greater force at work, and one with a very ironic sense of humour!

"Take the *girls* with you, and do what you can, whilst I hold the *fort* here."

It seemed as though he had little choice but to trust her, so nodding to the two young women, he picked up his Gladstone bag, opening it as Oracle jumped inside. Closing it quickly, they all left, walking back through her office and out into the corridor to wait for the lift. The bell pinged, but it was not the only thing to arrive. Sagittarius found himself smothered with hugs and kisses, as they were so relieved that their man had been rescued.

It was a bit of a struggle getting them into the lift, and as soon as he did, he pressed the button sending them down to the second floor.

It arrived with a slight jerk, which was just enough to prize them away from him. He did not have time for *that*, as he knew he would have to work quickly, before Special Agent Bond was overrun.

The corridor was plain white, just like all of the others in the building, with strong wooden doors in a light tone contrasting with the starkness. Each door was numbered, and as they moved along, he soon found room 205.

The plastic strip slotted neatly into the locking mechanism, and it instantly clicked open. Inside was nothing more than a storeroom, and as they slipped inside, the door closed firmly behind them.

Sagittarius could see a variety of things, uniforms, automatic weapons, and several boxes containing what he assumed to be part of his research. He moved towards the first box as the young women spoke to him.

"Oracle has reprogrammed us."

They spoke together.

"He also had the two taser guns hidden in his bag."

Sagittarius looked round, as they both began to remove their clothing. It appeared that Oracle had not done it well enough, as this was not the time or the place!

He quickly looked the other way, as two sets of large firm bare breasts pointed in his direction.

"We are going to change into these combat uniforms, whilst you find the cyber wasps."

That sounded good to him, as the last thing he felt like doing right now was to look at their half naked bodies. He reached over, opening the nearest box, which was just as well, as all they had on were minuscule *G strings!*

It was not the correct box, and as he closed it again, searching the next, they continued to dress.

He soon found the right box, which was about the size of a *tea chest.* Inside there was the main control unit, and layers of black and yellow striped *cyber wasps*, all packed neatly into a honeycomb of protective foam.

He clasped hold of the control unit, and as he turned round, he was greeted by two sets of cleavages. Even though they were both wearing black combat uniforms, they had left the front zippers half undone!

Sagittarius shook his head in disbelief and turned away, grabbing hold of his Gladstone bag. When he opened it, he looked sternly at Oracle, who just sat their like a picture of innocence. He would have to have a word with him when he had the chance!

Turning away from Oracle, he went back to the *stealth wasps*. Each one carried a small dose of nano robots, ready to be programmed. They could be injected into anyone they stung, and it looked as though Special Agent Bond's idea was for him to program them to seek and destroy the foreign nano robots.

This was a job for Oracle, who linked his processor to the control device via an infra-red transmitter hidden in his ears. He already carried all the information he needed, as he had successfully rendered the foreign nano robots useless on several occasions.

Sagittarius held the control device, as Oracle sent the programming sequence. The *girls* emptied the contents of their hand bags into their front pockets, before pulling on socks and boots. They then tied their hair back into tight pony tails, and donned black berets.

Even though they wore black combat uniforms, they still managed to look sexy. There was definitely something wrong with their hormones, which was something else that he would have to be deal with later!

Oracle severed the infra-red connection as the programming was complete, just as the two young women grabbed the automatic weapons, along with several bullet clips. They seemed to know exactly what they were doing, and armed their weapons, ready to move out. They had placed their clothes, hand bags and shoes into rucksacks, which each of them had slung over a shoulder.

Sagittarius grabbed the box, lifting out the first layer of protective foam. It was full of cyber wasps, who began to buzz as they came to life. On the ceiling there was the vent for the air conditioning, and they all rose, heading towards it.

It was quite a sight, as they flew between the spaces in the mesh grid, disappearing out of sight.

He placed the foam to one side, lifting up the next batch, which again began to buzz. In total there were a thousand stealth wasps, all fully operational and programmed to sting everyone in the building. It was a far cry from the Experimental Department, and he guessed that someone had been doing a lot of overtime lately!

When the last of them had disappeared, he placed the foam back in the box, along with the controller, and hid it in the corner, placing other boxes on top of it. When he was sure that he had hidden any evidence that they had been there, he opened the door.

The corridor was empty, as Gemini and Caprica moved out, followed by Sagittarius carrying Oracle, who was still in his bag.

Moving swiftly along they approached the lift, and the door *pinged*, opening slowly. Out walked a man carrying a set of files. He moved towards them, and his eyes instinctively settled on the cleavages of the *girls*. He was transfixed for a moment by the soft firm flesh, and did not notice a wasp suddenly emerge from the air conditioning vent above. It swooped down embedding its sting into the back of his neck.

The man looked round wondering what had happened, before stumbling and collapsing on the floor.

It appeared that the cyber wasps were working, and they left him there as they entered the lift.

99

Sagittarius pressed the button and the doors began to close, as they headed down to ground level.

# Fifteen

The moonlight shone down on the armoured column which had taken up position outside the SIS building, forming a *ring of steel*. It was not certain that they would be needed, although all Medical and Government buildings in the Capital were now guarded.

Sagittarius held the door open as Gemini and Caprica walked through looking very smart in their black uniforms. It was certainly quite a change from the flimsy summer dresses they had both been wearing earlier. Sagittarius felt a little more comfortable in their presence now, as not only had they proved themselves to be trustworthy, but also they were not quite so *intimidating*. It had been difficult keeping his eyes fixed on their faces, as he had no wish to show them any encouragement by a straying eye!

Security had been easy to pass, as the man on the door was getting used to seeing him, although now wearing black combat uniforms, the two young women did look a little different, and as they all calmly walked over towards the vehicles, an officer came over to greet them.

"Professor Brandon Sagittarius, Head of Experimental Department."

He showed the officer his identification, and the officer saluted.

"Captain Charlotte, Royal Corps of Signals."

Sagittarius froze.

He had not noticed that it was a female officer, but when he took a closer look, he could see that beneath the black beret there was a pretty face, and blonde hair tied back in a pony tail.

Her khaki camouflage uniform covered a trim figure and also appeared to conceal a healthy bust. In many ways she resembled Gemini and Caprica, particularly in the way she looked at him. For a moment he began to wonder if she was another *doppelgänger*?

She was of similar height, but thankfully her facial features were a little different. There was one similarity which he found uncomfortable, and that was the way she was looking at him. Her eyes seemed to be all over him, and after she had *inspected* him, he got the distinct impression that she found him equally as attractive as the two young women standing behind him did. There followed an awkward pause before he spoke again.

"We need to get to GCHQ (Government Communications Headquarters) in Cheltenham, and it is a matter of some urgency."

The Captain continued to look at him and his two companions.

"Oh, that is myself, Gemini and Caprica."

She looked at the two women, thinking that he was using their code names.

"In fact, it is a matter of *National Security*."

Those two words always unlocked a lot of doors, and on this occasion it proved to be no exception.

"I will have to check with my Commanding Officer."

With that she saluted again, and left, returning to the vehicles. Sagittarius hoped that they would be able to spare a vehicle and a driver, otherwise they were going to find it very difficult to get there, and to get past whatever obstacles they might encounter.

It did not take her long to return, and when she did he was very surprised by what she said.

"My Commanding Office thinks that it would be a good idea if I accompany you, as I am an Officer in the Signals."

She then pointed towards an Armoured Personnel Carrier which sat at the front of the column.

"It would be best if we use the *Saxon*, as you never know what we might encounter on our journey."

The Saxon was a squat, square looking vehicle, with four thick tyres protruding from the camouflaged green paintwork. On top there was a machine gun, which he hoped they would not need to use.

They all moved forward, and when they walked to the rear, she opened the double doors, indicating for them to enter.

Inside was quite spacious, with a long green topped seat on either side, which led to the platform for the gunner. Beyond that was the driver's seat Sagittarius helped Gemini and Caprica up, before extending a hand to the Captain. She smiled, not being used to that in the army. Today everyone was treated as an equal, and there were already quite a lot of female members of the Signal Corps.

She accepted his hand, and as he climbed up after her, she leaned over, brushing her chest against him and looked deep into his eyes as she closed the doors. It was quite clear that it was intentional, and he began to wonder just what it was about him that was having this effect on women. He looked at his Gladstone bag, where Oracle was sitting innocently inside, Sagittarius wondered if he had anything to do with it?

Gemini and Caprica strapped themselves in as he followed the Captain, leaving Oracle in their capable hands. The front seat was also green, and as she climbed into position, he stood behind her in the well by the side door.

The ignition brought the engine to life, and he swayed, holding onto the side as they pulled forward, smiling to himself. It was quite Surreal riding in an Armoured Personnel Carrier, and his thoughts drifted back to another one of his childhood favourite series - *Captain Scarlet and the Mysterons.* In particular he thought of the *Special Patrol Vehicle* which was one of the things they travelled in, a model of which he still had at home. Instead of Captain Scarlet in an SPV, it was Captain Charlotte in an APC!

It was also coincidental that in the series there were captains with the code names of colours, whereas in this scenario it was astrological names. Also, Captain Scarlet was indestructible and rapidly healed from his wounds, in the same way that he had healed from his own bullet wound. The enemy was the Mysterons from Mars, although he doubted whether the Organisation was *Martian.* Captain Scarlet may have had nano robots inside his body though, and that thought lingered as he looked at Captain Charlotte.

"Have you had the *Bat Flu* vaccine yet?"

She looked over her shoulder towards him, as she steered the Saxon past a few parked cars.

"No, I have just been recalled from leave, and there wasn't time to visit the M.O."

Sagittarius breathed out a huge sigh of relief.

104

It appeared that a few people were slipping through the net, and he had to get to GCHQ before the *net* tightened.

"What I am about to tell you is highly classified, and may seem more than a little strange, but it is the reason that we must get to Cheltenham."

She looked at him again, and he wondered if she was still going to be quite so *enthusiastic* about him when he told her the truth. It was a gamble, but one he felt as though he had no choice but to take, as her security clearance and undoubted skills in the field of communications would prove to be invaluable.

"Well, have you ever wondered about the possibility of nano technology?"

There was a brief pause before she answered.

"As a matter of fact, I have recently come back from a course, where that very subject was part of the program. Everything is getting smaller all of the time, and with the communications and computer systems we now have, I can see the day when most devices are minuscule"

That was the best news that he had had for along time and he responded.

"Well, I am in charge of the Experimental Department at MI6, where we have been developing some quite remarkable stuff, and nano technology is amongst it."

He took a brief pause, as he tried to make everything sound plausible.

"Some of our developments have fallen into the wrong hands. Nano technology can be used to influence behaviour, and if injected into the body, it can affect the brain. Once inside, a signal can be sent, and anyone can effectively be controlled."

That sounded very futuristic, and he hoped by informing her of his role within MI6, that she would think he was credible.

"Sounds frightening!"

He looked at her.

"Well, it is more frightening than you realise."

The Captain looked worried.

"I'm afraid that things are very serious, very serious indeed."

She kept her eyes on the road, as they drove through a normally busy intersection. Everywhere was unnaturally quiet, but she kept her eyes *peeled* nevertheless.

"From what we understand, there is a group calling themselves the *Organisation*. They have acquired the technology to inject a lot of people with nano robots, and have the means of controlling them via some privately funded communication satellites. You may have heard of the latest launch a few days ago?"

She nodded, having caught that particular news bulletin before attention had been focussed on the approaching crisis.

"Now, the *Bat Flu* pandemic is a cover story for them to inject a carefully chosen few with these nano robots, and the rest will be injected with the virus, which will take the lives of hundreds of thousands, if not millions of innocent people."

The Saxon swerved slightly, as the enormity of what he was saying began to sink in.

"I know it all sounds very *far-fetched*, but the Department, Government, and possibly the Military may have already been compromised!"

The Captain looked at him in disbelief.

"Have you heard of any *Bat Flu* cases?"

She thought about it for a moment.

"Only a couple of people the media said were being treated in a London clinic."

"Precisely!"

Sagittarius was making headway.

"Surely the hospitals would be full of sick people by now."

He was right, there had hardly been any ambulance sirens for hours, and few Police ones either.

"We need to get to Cheltenham, as it is the only facility which possesses the right equipment to jam the signal. If we don't succeed, then there will be no stopping them!"

Captain Charlotte, although sceptical, could see the logic in what he was saying. He did have identification, had emerged from the SIS building, and did look and speak like an intelligent man. The two young women with him were wearing Black Operations uniforms, and she had wondered where all of the sick people were.

"It is not going to be easy, but with your help, we stand a chance."

There was silence, as she thought about all that he had said.

For a start, it did appeal to her natural spirit of adventure, which was the main reason she had joined the army in the first place. Then, as she studied him from her rear view mirror, she had to admit that he was a handsome, smartly dressed man who could quite easily pass as a *Secret Agent*. There was definitely something *different* about him, which was difficult to put her proverbial *finger* on.

It was not just what he had said, but the way he had said it. His presence was having quite an effect upon her, and she could feel herself flush as the inside of the Saxon suddenly felt uncomfortably warm.

It was as though the nano robots were already inside her body, and playing havoc with her senses. Her hormones seemed to be all over the place, and before she knew what she was doing, Captain Charlotte reached behind her seat with her left hand, grabbing the back of his thigh, giving it a gentle squeeze.

"I would like to go all the way with you!"

Sagittarius's face went bright red, as he noticed the dazed expression on her face as she turned and smiled at him.

"...to Cheltenham, and to help you block the satellite signal."

He had a feeling that somehow she had other things on her mind...

# Sixteen

Oracle sat in his Gladstone bag feeling rather pleased with himself, as he continued to influence the Captain. She was correct in what she had stated, that she had not received a vaccination; therefore, there were no foreign nano robots within her body. Fortunately, she had arrived back on duty too late for the Medical Officer to inject her, although he suspected that it would only be a matter of time before they caught up with her.

He already had a wealth of information on the subject, and had discovered that whenever anyone had been injected, then the foreign nano robots had some noticeable side effects. Apart from controlling behaviour, they also had an effect on the body's natural hormone levels. Men had a much higher level of testosterone, which made them far more aggressive than they would normally be, and strangely, it was also the case in women too!

A woman has a moderate level of testosterone which naturally occurs within her body, and by increasing the level significantly, she would lose her femininity. A man also has oestrogen, and Oracle had discovered that by boosting the levels in both sexes, it had a significant effect on the foreign nano robots.

Oracle was able to transmit extremely low frequency waves via the transmitter buried inside Sagittarius's fob watch. These waves went directly to the subconscious mind, mimicking the body's own electromagnetic signals, which naturally fire along the neuron pathways. By doing this, he was able to increase the oestrogen levels within both sexes.

He had also worked out that increasing the oestrogen levels confused the foreign nano robots to a certain extent, disguising the fact that someone had not received a vaccination. In this way he hoped that it would aid them on their mission to GCHQ.

There was only one slight problem, and that was the fact that it was having a *certain effect* on the women that Sagittarius was encountering!

Captain Charlotte removed her left hand, as they went around a tight corner, and he took the opportunity to turn around and sit on the seat behind her facing the back of the vehicle. Gemini and Caprica both looked at him with adoring eyes, making him feel even more uncomfortable, and it looked as though it was going to be a long drive to Cheltenham!

Oracle could sense how uncomfortable the Captain's attention was making Sagittarius feel, and despite being a *cyber rabbit*, he managed to produce the slightest of mischievous grins. Big Jim had been working on his emotional responses, and he was beginning to develop a personality of his own. It was a good job that Sagittarius could not see him, otherwise he would have been shocked. *Cyber rabbits* were not supposed to have that ability!

Oracle was quickly learning about human behaviour, and had begun to mimic it quite successfully. He had, however, kept that to himself but, unbeknown to anyone, he started to grin again. He found Sagittarius's plight really amusing, as he was trapped in here for the next two hours!

The London streets were unusually quiet, as most people had returned to their homes, and all public transport had been cancelled as the curfew deadline approached. The only activity was from the odd police or ambulance vehicle, and those from the army, who were still taking up positions around the city. It was uncomfortably quiet, as even the sound of aircraft overhead had ceased, as the full restrictions came into place. The city was in effect in *lock down*, as everyone waited for the next Government announcement.

Inside the armoured personnel carrier, the situation was also tense, but for a different reason. Oracle's manipulation of the oestrogen levels of the three women had led to a sexual tension within its protective steel shell. Sagittarius was still trapped in his seat, having to deal with the Captain's straying hands, and it was with some relief that they arrived at a check point on the outskirts of the city.

Captain Charlotte pulled the vehicle to one side, as a group of armed soldiers appeared from behind a makeshift barricade. They had guns poised, although being an army vehicle, they assumed that it was on official business.

Sagittarius stood up, turning to see why she had stopped, and as he did so, she unfastened her seat belt, climbing over the back of her seat, stumbling and grabbing hold of him. Her face came to rest just in front of his, with her lips poised over his.

She looked as though she was about to kiss him, as they heard a shout from outside.

"Halt, who goes there!"

It was just enough to distract her, and he managed to move away, although she was able to deliberately brush her chest against him again, as she joined him in the well by the side door.

The Captain was like one big walking hormone, as she struggled to control herself. Her behaviour was not at all like an officer of the Signal Corps, and it looked as though something was indeed affecting her. Oracle gave another grin from inside his Gladstone bag, as he too was acting completely out of character.

When she slid the door aside, they were met by a soldier holding a rifle. He looked a little surprised to see a suited man standing there next to the Captain. Fortunately she spoke first, and what she said seemed to ease the tension.

"I am Captain Charlotte of the Signal Corps, and this is Professor Sagittarius of MI6. We are on our way to GCHQ on a very important mission."

Very slowly, they both stepped down onto the tarmac, and Sagittarius reached into his inside pocket removing his identification, which he showed to the soldier. Another soldier covered him as he examined it, with the aid of the street lights which shone down brightly from above.

"Everything seems to be in order."

Sagittarius felt relieved, as he had had quite enough of being confronted by armed men for one day!

"Do you mind if I check the back?"

The Captain left him standing there, as she stepped out of the Saxon and moved towards the rear of the vehicle, opening the double doors. Inside Gemini and Caprica sat innocently, smiling at the soldier as he studied them. They were wearing their black combat uniforms which seemed to fit the scenario, although the soldier did wonder why the Professor was accompanied by such attractive young women!

Sagittarius had a few very uncomfortable moments until they were finally on their way, none more so than when they both re-entered the Saxon. The Captain tried to kiss him again, as her hormones seemed to be all over the place. All of this unwanted female attention was starting to get to him, and there seemed to be only one logical explanation.

Taking hold of his Gladstone bag, he opened it, staring accusingly at the large black rabbit sitting inside.

Oracle sat there like a picture of innocence, although when he was closing the bag, Sagittarius thought that he saw a grin appearing on his face. Maybe he was imagining things, but there was definitely something unusual about the way Oracle was acting!

# Seventeen

The sound of the engine seemed to drone on relentlessly as the armoured personnel carrier trundled along through the mostly deserted streets. Everywhere seemed to have an eerie calm, and there was definitely something in the air. It was as though the populations subconscious minds were all grouped together, somehow sensing that something was not quite right.

Sagittarius had the same feeling, and it was not just about what was planned to start in the morning. The vaccination program had to be stopped and the satellite transmission blocked. He knew that, but there was something else niggling at the back of his mind.

For what seemed like days, there had been a continuous stream of unexplained coincidences, people with strange names, and even stranger behaviour. Who would have thought that there would have been a Special Agent going by the name of *Bond?*

It was truly bizarre!

Then, how she had suddenly changed, although if she was a *Special Agent* then she had to be good!

No, it was not that so much, or the fact that he had encountered his *doppelgänger* again, or the Doctor, or even Taurus for that matter. Something else still did not seem to add up!

Sitting there in contemplation opposite the *girls*, who seemed to be quite contented that he was now back with them, he looked over towards the Captain. She was less contented, as he was now out of *fondling range*. It was not the fact that he had three very hormonal women to deal with, it was just something odd about the suited men. The more that he thought about them, the more he wished that he had punched the younger one, who had been doing all of the talking. Taking their own lives had been extreme, although judging by what they had planned, maybe it was not quite so surprising?

Tapping his fingers gently on the seat next to him, he visualised them sitting there. It was very odd that the older one never spoke during the whole time he had been in the room with them. Now, that was very unusual!

He had also sensed that there was an external presence, and that was also bugging him.

Bug was, however, a very appropriate term, for there was indeed another presence hidden somewhere in the background, a presence that had indeed placed a bug within the room.

Sitting observing through a set of monitors, *Dark Star* had watched and listened to everything that had taken place. Losing the two suited men had been a setback, although there were still a lot more Organisation members scattered around the city. Making contact with them formed part of *plan B*, as the Organisation never took anything for granted.

*Dark Star* passed the information onto the next contact on the list via a discreet text, bounced off several fictitious accounts. It was vital that control was maintained, as the vaccination program was due to commence in just a few short hours.

Information was also being received suggesting that there was a problem with the nano robots. Some of them had stopped functioning, and it looked as though there was an unknown force combating them. It was difficult to tell what it was, although the internal security cameras within the SIS building had shown that a few people had collapsed.

This information was also relayed, as well as a request for a squad of men to be sent to re-inject them. It also appeared that the Personal Assistant had shown her true colours, being a *double agent*. Information about her had also been passed on, and steps would be taken to deal with her too!

*Special Agent Bond* was not acting alone, and the Professor was far more resourceful than anyone had given him credit for. These were minor setbacks though, as like an experienced card player, *Dark Star* was yet to play his full hand…

# Eighteen

The cloudless sky brought a chill to the air, as the full moon shone down in all of its glory, almost turning night into day. For centuries, it had caused those of a *nervous disposition* many a sleepless night, as it had been associated with *witches* and *werewolves. Shakespeare's moon-struck madness* had been written about it, and even the word *lunacy* derived from its negative connotations.

Secure in the Armoured Personnel Carrier, Sagittarius stared up at it from his position in the gunner's turret. He was standing with his head poking through the open hatch, taking some air as the monotonous droning of the engine had made him feel quite drowsy. It had not been too bad whilst they had been travelling along the M40, but now that they were on the A40, the country air seemed unusually heavy.

Captain Charlotte slowed as they approached a set of traffic lights, which seemed to be in the middle of nowhere. There was not a soul about, and all had been quiet, apart from a passing military convoy she had flashed her lights too, which had been going in the opposite direction.

There was just something unnerving about the sight of the full moon, particularly on a night like this, where everything was so remarkably still. There was not even the hint of a breeze as they ground to a halt, and he could well imagine where all the superstitions came from. It was enough to make his skin crawl, and as he shivered, the unearthly cry of a fox calling for his mate nearly made him jump out of his proverbial *skin.*

"Auuuh!"

Sagittarius jumped, banging the back of his head against the turret's protective cover. Feeling rather foolish, he stepped down, closing the cover behind him!

If he was going to tackle matters at GCHQ, then he really had to pull himself together. The foreign nano robots had really unsettled him again, and he was thankful that his own had all but cleared them from his system.

Gemini and Caprica were both asleep, cuddled up together, as he knelt on the seat behind the Captain, looking over her shoulder and out through the bullet proof glass of the small driving window.

She sensed his presence, and moved her left arm, grabbed the back of his thigh again, giving it a gentle squeeze.

"What are we going to do when we reach GCHQ?"

That was a good question!

He had been running various scenarios through his mind, which was another reason for getting some fresh air to clear his head.

"I am not really sure!"

He felt the pressure lessen.

"We will be their in less than half an hour, so you had better get a *grip* on things."

With that she moved her hand up towards his backside, giving his left buttock the *hand treatment*.

Inside his bag, Oracle grinned, increasing her oestrogen level again.

"We will have to ascertain whether or not the facility has also been compromised, and if there are any other agents on our side."

That was going to be easier said than done, as it was a large complex manned by several thousand people. It was a complete contrast to the dreamy spires of Oxford, which they had passed what seemed like hours ago. That was a different sort of intelligence centre, and one which he had been part of many years ago.

The outskirts of Cheltenham seemed deserted as they drove on towards the town, nearing their destination.

The GCHQ building was shaped like a large doughnut, with three curved pieces which sat equidistantly on top, giving it the appearance of a wheel. There were also four other building with the same smooth metallic finish, that sat around the sides in amongst the car parking facilities, within the perimeter fence.

There was open countryside to one side, and housing developments and a host of other buildings on the others, none of which they could see clearly from the level ground they were travelling across.

The A40 wound its way into the outskirts of Cheltenham, where they were met by checkpoint, manned by a small detachment of armed troops. It was the same procedure as before, only this time Sagittarius was wise to the advances of the Captain, standing well back as she left her seat!

It did not do much good, because she got him on the way back, pressing him tightly against the inside of the vehicle as she closed the outer door. It was worrying to see a female officer so out of control, especially as they were undertaking a mission of so much importance.

She held his arms down by his sides, as she planted a big kiss on his lips.

"I have wanted to do that all night!"

Sagittarius knew that already, and was relieved when she let him go!

Although she looked feminine, she had a rather masculine grip, and he suspected that she could be some sort of a *martial arts* expert. That would come in handy when they were inside GCHQ, however, it was just arriving safely that was now his major concern!

Fortunately, the rest of their journey was quite uneventful, with the two young women sitting quietly together, without the slightest hint of jealousy at what they both must have witnessed. There was clearly something wrong with all of them, but not as wrong as the whole situation he found himself in.

There was no time for contemplation however, as the time for action had arrived!

Staring out of the driver's front window he could see movement up ahead and, as they got closer, they could clearly see an armed convoy. It consisted of several armoured personnel carriers, tanks and quite a lot of heavily armed troops guarding the main entrance. He also suspected that the long perimeter fence was also ringed with *steel*, and it looked more like they were expecting a war rather than a *pandemic*.

Security was tight, far tighter than it had been at either of the checkpoints, and the Captain made sure that the *girls'* uniforms were being worn correctly, without the slightest hint of cleavage. When they all climbed down, the three women stood and saluted an officer who came marching towards them, accompanied by a small squad of heavily armed soldiers.

Papers were scrutinised and the vehicle checked, with nothing more suspicious found than what looked like a doctor's bag with a large black rabbit sitting inside. At first the soldiers did not know what to think of Oracle, but the officer seemed to find the explanation plausible, that they were going to test whether the *Bat Flu* virus could be passed on to other creatures, even though he thought it odd that the rabbit was not in a cage.

Sagittarius went on to explain that it would be better for the *girls* to remain with the rabbit in the *Saxon* until they were needed. He could see by the look on their faces that they both wished to hug and kiss him, and ask him to be careful, but there was nothing that they could do but leave him in the *capable hands* of the Captain.

So, it was just the two of them who were escorted to the main door by an army Land Rover, and as they travelled towards it they could see that there seemed to be a lot of activity everywhere.

When the engine stopped, they were escorted out, and taken directly to security. It was similar to that of the SIS building, although the security guard did not recognise him, as he had only ever been here once before.

Inside the green glass and steel shell, there were cafés, bars a restaurant and a gym, as well as the various departments, all linked by an internal street which ran all the way around the inside of the *doughnut*. It was so long that it would take more than five minutes to walk around. In the basement an electric goods train ran around delivering items, as well as an underground road which handled the more *sensitive* material. In some ways it was more like a self contained village, with the computer room the size of a small football stadium. It was staggering to think that there were five thousand miles of cabling, with just the one needing to be found to stop the transmission of the rogue satellite system!

The walkway ran between two open tiers, and their boots echoed on the polished tiled floor as the walked along unchallenged. Somehow they were going to have to find the main computer room, and the right terminal within it. Obviously there was someone operating it covertly, but with so many people working here, it was not going to be an easy task locating them.

Sagittarius stopped for a moment, checking his watch. He did not wish to know the time, but to release another one of his stealth flies. It quickly emerged, flying off as he clipped the fastening back into position, nonchalantly placing it back in his jacket pocket as they continued to walk.

The fly instantly started transmitting data, which Oracle received in the Armoured Personnel Carrier. He was already getting a multitude of readings from the building, and in amongst them, there was the unmistakeable signature of foreign nano robots.

It looked as though part, if not all of GCHQ had also been compromised, and things did not look good, not good at all!

Oracle managed to bring up some schematics of the building onto the inside of Sagittarius's glasses, and he could see exactly where the very large computer room was. He could also see a café through the transparent lenses, which made him feel hungry and thirsty. It was hours since he had any refreshment, and even the lingering smells of stale coffee did not put him off.

GCHQ ran on a twenty four hour basis, and even though it was in the middle of the night, there were still some people grabbing a little something.

"Do you mind if we stop for refreshments?"

The Captain nodded her head.

"I'd love a *quickie!*"

Sagittarius took that as a *yes*, even thought it had other connotations!

Everything and everyone seemed upside down, and no one seemed to be acting normally any more. The world seemed to have gone mad, or at least the people he had encountered.

They moved to the counter, as the fly hovered a discrete distance above, and he ordered a fruit juice. The Captain asked for one too, much to his relief. The last thing that he wished for was *coffee breath*!

The man behind the counter got them their drinks, and Sagittarius could not help but notice how effeminate he was. He slipped his hand into his pocket, pulling out a five pound note and handing it over.

"Keep the change!"

The man winked at him puckering his lips, making him feel very uncomfortable.

Back in the Armoured Personnel Carrier, Oracle grinned, and for the first time in his life managed the smallest of *titters.*

The Captain was not impressed, and slipped her arm into his, as the man looked away in disgust. She then guided Sagittarius towards a table, and sat him down quickly.

The juice was cool and refreshing, and as they sat there, they noticed two security guards doing their rounds. Security was obviously tight, and they pretended not to notice the two uniformed men as they approached the café. However, the security men had noticed them.

They were armed, which was most unusual, and Sagittarius instantly knew that there was something wrong. Any hopes that they would simply walk past were quickly dashed as they made their way over, stopping at their table.

"Professor Sagittarius, Captain Charlotte, your presence is requested."

He suspected that it would not be for a friendly chat!

Everything seemed to be revolving around in one big ever decreasing circle of capture and escape.

So, quickly finishing their drinks, they got up slowly from the table. There seemed little point in resisting as if they did, then it would make their task even more difficult.

The men pointed to the walkway, and they moved back towards it, being ushered along at the point of a gun. The security men had that certain *look* about them, which he suspected was due to the foreign nano robots controlling them, and it also looked as though their luck was finally beginning to run out!

At least the fly was still active, and Oracle and the *girls* were safe inside the Saxon. He had a plan B, Sagittarius always had a *plan B!*

*Plan A* now took them towards a solid wooden door on the ground floor, and as they approached the door opened, and there standing grinning was the younger suited man!

Sagittarius was shocked to see him, as he thought that he had taken a cyanide pill and died at the SIS building. Things were getting even more bizarre, and when they entered the room, there was the older suited man sitting behind a desk. It was déjà vu all over again!

"Welcome to GCHQ, Professor!"

It was not much of a welcome as he was forced into a chair, just like before. This time however, he made sure that it did not contain restraints.

"We should stop meeting like this!"

For the first time the older suited man spoke, in another very posh sounding voice.

"You are becoming a bit of a nuisance!"

Sagittarius was not pleased to see him either!

"We lost two good *doppelgänger* because of you, although the one resembling me could not quite get the accent right."

So that was why he never spoke!

At least that was one mystery solved, although it created another. Just how many *doppelgänger* did they have, and were these the real two or not?

"I am afraid that your little plan has failed. Special Agent Bond has now been captured, and control of the SIS building has been re-established."

His heart sank.

"Nice little try with the stealth wasps, you are indeed a very versatile man!"

If what he was saying was true, then it looked as if things were over. There was no way that they were going to get to the main computer room, and even if they did, it would only be a matter of time before the Organisation found another way of activating the satellite system.

"Your resourcefulness is to be admired."

Sagittarius slowly slipped his hand into his inside pocket, pulling out his fob watch.

"Yes Professor, time has run out."

It was not the time that he was looking at, although as he did glance at the dial, it indicated that the new day was about to dawn, and with it the lifting of the curfew. The vaccination program would then start, followed by the pandemic!

"Such a pity that you did not decide to join us."

Sagittarius had no regrets.

"I am afraid that you both will have to die!"

With that, the security men took silencers out of their pockets, screwing them onto the barrels of their revolvers.

Captain Charlotte looked at him, reaching over putting her arms around him.

"How touching - you certainly have your way with the ladies."

He whispered something into her ear, as they embraced.

"And now if you will excuse us, we have important business to attend too."

126

With that, the two suited men left the room, as the security guards aimed their weapons.

The door to the room then closed, and as it did so, there was the muffled sound of two bullets being fired, followed by silence...

# Nineteen

A blinding flash of light filled the room, as Sagittarius and Captain Charlotte threw themselves to the ground. The security guards could not see a thing and fired instinctively. There was a pause, and then the sound of them both falling to the ground.

"OK!"

Sagittarius, after counting to ten, gave the signal for them to open their eyes.

Both men had been shot, and having missed their protective flack jackets, each one had shot the other in their firing arm. The Captain quickly gathered their weapons, as Sagittarius reached inside his jacket pocket. He pulled out what looked like a spectacle case, and as he opened it, there were several hypodermic needles inside.

With the Captain giving cover, he injected both men with friendly nano robots, which would not only combat the foreign nano robots which controlled them, but also heal their bullet wounds. He then laid them out on their sides in the *recovery position* as they lost consciousness.

The Captain lowered her gun, wrapping her arms around him, and kissing him passionately. He had saved both of their lives by activating the flare housed within his fob watch. Sometimes being Head of Experimental Department came in handy!

Eventually, the Captain had to surface for air, and when she did, he took the opportunity to break free.

"Oh, Professor!"

She was about to kiss him again, when he put his hand up.

"We still have to stop the satellite transmission."

She kissed him again anyway!

Eventually, he managed to break free, and they each slipped a weapon into their belts, before moving to the doorway. Peering out, the coast appeared to be clear, and the fly, which had been waiting patiently outside the room for them, began to guide them towards the main computer room.

The passage was long and stretched downwards under the road which ran around the outside of the *doughnut*. It was guarded by some soldiers, who saluted their superior officer, and the Captain saluted back.

"So far, so good!"

Sagittarius was pleased that they were now making good progress, and as they hurried along, the corridor began to rise.

Up ahead there were yet more troops, who were guarding a large set of solid wooden doors. It certainly looked as though things were *hotting up*, as the level of security was far greater than he remembered from before. They were also armed, which again was very unusual, and he hoped that the Captain would be able to get them through into the main computer room.

Captain Charlotte saluted, and the three soldiers on duty saluted back. She then briefly explained that she was here escorting the Professor, who showed them his MI6 identification. That seemed to suffice, and they were granted entry.

The main computer room was absolutely enormous, with more electronic equipment than either of them had ever seen in one place before. It looked like an endless stream of terminals, sweeping out into a river of knowledge. Each operator was

129

engrossed in their particular given task, and coordinating all of them must have been a logistical nightmare!

Trying to find the exact terminal that was controlling the satellite transmission was going to be like trying to find the proverbial *needle in a haystack.*

Maybe they should have tried to hack into the system?

That was a good idea in principle, but in practice, it would be virtually impossible, and even if they did succeed, it really needed someone here to show a physical presence. With all of these computer experts, any deviation from the transmission would only be temporary, as there were people who could still reactivate it.

There was, however, one talented computer hacker, who had already gained access to the system.

*Dark star* was a computer genius, and had been able to manipulate the system, coming into the Organisation half way through *The Plan*. The nano robots had already been perfected, and all that was needed was someone with the knowledge to link them to the satellite network. The network had already been nearly fully operational too, and it was just a certain little *something* they lacked to make the whole system complete.

Hidden in the shadows, the secretive figure watched from a hidden device, secretly planted within the room, as had several others within the whole building. On the screen, it showed Sagittarius and Captain Charlotte, as they stood by the doorway, looking out towards the multitude of computer terminals.

GCHQ was supposed to be the intelligence and security organisation that kept the British Isles safe from outside threats. However, it was an inside threat that was causing all of the problems at the moment!

GCHQ dated back from *Bletchley Park*, the *World War II* site that decoded the German *Enigma* machine which held all of their secret codes. Ironically, it was Sagittarius's grandfather who had played a part, and now he was standing in the very hub.

Being part of the government, and also MI5 and the Secret Intelligence Service (MI6), it was quite natural for Sagittarius to be there. What was unnatural however, was the Organisation which had infiltrated it, and the nano robots who controlled a majority of the staff.

GCHQ was here to combat the *cyber threat* posed from terrorists groups, foreign states and criminals, as well as the threat posed by espionage. The Organisation covered all of these things, and now that it had infiltrated the whole establishment, it was poised to do what had never been done before!

Some people looked over to where they were standing, wondering what they were going to do. Sagittarius was also wondering the same thing, as they had not got much time. The fly had followed them, and was busily relaying information back to Oracle. It was not the only signal, as it had picked up a dramatic increase in the testosterone level. With so many people in such a close proximity, the foreign nano robots were having an effect of both him and the Captain.

Her facial features began to change, and he could feel a distinct hardening of her attitude towards him. That was not such as bad thing, as her amorous behaviour had been making him feel more than a little uncomfortable. Things were about to take a significant change for the worse, as the door suddenly opened, and there stood Gemini and Caprica.

They looked at the Captain, who stared back at them, and there was definitely a mounting tension between them.

At first Sagittarius thought that they had come to offer their assistance, and could see his Gladstone bag in Gemini's hand. He had asked them to stay in the Saxon, but he presumed that Oracle had changed his plan.

There was an awkward silence as the three women stared at each other, with their testosterone levels increasing all of the time. He could sense that something was about to happen, and as Gemini placed the bag down on the floor, both young women spoke at once.

"Get your hands off our man!"

Sagittarius looked astonished, as confrontation loomed. He had been surprised that nothing had happened earlier, as all three of them seemed to have *designs* on him.

"He's mine!"

Captain Charlotte replied, and they all squared up to one another before he could do anything, a scuffle broke out.

The very unseemly exhibition of three women grappling with each other caused everyone to look round, and Sagittarius wished that the ground would literally *open up* and swallow him. What no one noticed however, was that Oracle had opened the escape hatch in the side of his bag, and had scurried away under the cover of the distraction.

The soldiers who had been guarding the door, opened it, wondering what all of the noise was about. They also stared in disbelief at the sight of a Signals Captain brawling with two other soldiers of a lower rank.

Oracle hopped towards the centre of the room, his processor having already identified which computer station was responsible for transmitting the satellite signal.

The man who was operating it felt a sharp jab in his ankle, as Oracle sank his sharp front teeth into him. The friendly nano robots quickly entering his blood stream, as he looked down to see a black rabbit standing on his hind legs. Oracle then transmitted a computer virus created by Big Jim, via an infra-red signal generated by his processor, which shot out of his ears.

The computer screen suddenly went *haywire*, showing a random set of number which formed a *zigzag* pattern. The operator did not know what to do, as his vision blurred and he began to feel very light headed.

Oracle then shot off, hopping under the desks and dodging the multitude of wires, as he made his way back towards his Gladstone bag.

When he arrived, the soldiers were just breaking up the fight, and no one noticed him slipping back through the escape hatch.

Sagittarius had never been so embarrassed in all of his life, and the thought of three women fighting over him, not to mention making such an exhibition of themselves in public, was something that he found appalling.

He was not the only one, as security had arrived, removed their weapons, and led all three of them away. If that was not bad enough, the security men also ushered him away too. It looked

133

as though he had failed, and been let down by very people he thought he could rely upon!

He looked at them with disgust, not realising that Oracle had planned the whole think. He had needed a diversion, and once he had received the computer virus, and identified which was the correct terminal, he had put his plan into action. He also calculated that it would take at least half an hour for the effects of the transmission to have worn off, and hoped that by the time that they reached where they were being taken, all would be clear.

The corridor seemed endless, as they were all ushered along, with Sagittarius carrying his bag, minus the gun he had taken from the security men, still not knowing what had been going on. He was not that comfortable with women at the best of times, and this episode had done nothing to change his opinion. The security men also looked at them with disgust, as their testosterone levels began to drop.

Three solemn faces looked at him, as a feeling of deep guilt began to spread through them. They did not understand why they had acted in the way that they had, and each one now realised that by the look on his face, they had probably lost the very thing they had been fighting over.

The end of the corridor led back to the main walkway, and from there they all proceeded to a security room, which lay just around the corner. They had not only lost the man that they all wanted, but the plan to stop the Organisation had also failed. Their guilt knew no bounds!

Once inside, they were each shown to a seat, and sat down with an air of resignation. The military took a very dim view of this sort of behaviour, and striking a senior officer would have resulted in several charges, if they had been real soldiers. No one knew that they were not, and both Gemini and Caprica feared the worst. They had nothing apart from Sagittarius, and without him destitution loomed!

If that was not bad enough, their cover would soon be blown, as the fake identification which they carried was bound to be revealed, only adding to their situation. It would be a matter for the Military Police, and both Gemini and Caprica also feared that they may be carted off to a military prison.

They all looked at Sagittarius, feeling rather foolish, and hoping that he would speak up for them. He looked so disgusted, as if he had *washed his hands* off them altogether. Without his testimony, they would be in very serious trouble indeed. They both looked at each other, having the same thought. Would they be classified as spies?

That thought sent a shock wave through their bodies, because if they were, then rumour had it that they shot spies - they both went very pale at the thought!

Captain Charlotte also felt terrible, and equally faced charges, and possibly a demotion. She had worked really hard to gain her rank, and now faced losing it over a brawl in GCHQ - she could not have chosen a worse place!

Their hormones had been all over the place, and none of them realised that their recent behaviour had all been down to a *cyber rabbit* who sat there innocently concealed in a Gladstone bag. It was a real pity as they had been so close to stopping the Organisation, which now appeared to have won.

Sagittarius did not seem too impressed, and by the unmistakable look on his face, they doubted whether he was ever going to forgive them. His mood changed for the worse as the door opened, and in walked the two suited men!

"You are becoming a bit of a nuisance, Professor!"

He looked at them with disgust too!

"We hoped that we had seen the last of you."

The feeling was mutual!

"Your little plan has failed again, and in only a few short hours we will have begun to take over completely."

Sagittarius sighed, realising that what they were saying was true. There was no way anyone could stop them now, and it also looked as though his fate had been sealed too. He was out of luck, and out of tricks, having used up all of his secret devices. His last hope was Oracle, who he doubted would be able to come to his rescue now, and even if he did, there was no point in fighting the inevitable.

Things looked grim!

"You seem to have more lives than the proverbial *cat* Professor, but now even you are not going to be able to get out of this one!"

It was the older suited man who spoke this time, and his cultured voice belayed a ruthless character whose evil intent knew no bounds!

From his inside pocket he produced a revolver, which he pointed at Sagittarius's head. *Revolver* seemed to be a reoccurring theme, as not only had one been pointed at his head before, but also the communication satellites that were transmitting the signal to the nano robots were *revolving* around the planet, probably passing over their heads at that very moment.

"They say that if you want a job doing well, then you have to do it yourself."

With that, he held the revolver with his finger poised over the trigger and looked ready to fire.

The three women looked horrified, realising that he was about to execute the man they all thought they loved.

Instinctively Captain Charlotte went to make a lunge, but before she got very far, she too felt the barrel of a gun. One of the security men had drawn his pistol, and it was now pressed to the back of her head. The other one had also drawn his, and that was now pointing towards Gemini and Caprica.

They all froze, as this looked like the end for all of them!

The older suited man gave a big smirk, as they closed their eyes, not wanting to witness what was about to happen.

Their worse fear was then realised, as a shot rang out!

# Twenty

An eerie mist swirled around the North Yorkshire Moors high above Harrogate, as the sun competed with the moon to bathe it with light. The scene resembled something you might have expected to see in a horror film, although this situation was very real.

Shrouded in secrecy, thirty giant golf balls, known as *radomes*, rose from the US military base at *Menwith Hill*. To anyone who did not know any better, it almost looked as if some mythical giant was about to swing a mighty club at them, sending them high up into the cloudless sky towards a distant flag.

Usually, they could be seen for miles around, and those that knew the base was there also knew that they, as well as *Menwith Hill*, were shrouded in secrecy.

The base had a direct link to the headquarters of the US National Security Agency (NSA) at Fort Mead in Maryland, as well as being linked to a series of other listening posts scattered across the world, including Britain's own GCHQ.

Every international telephone call, fax, e-mail, or radio transmission could be listened to by powerful computers capable of voice recognition. They homed in on a long list of key words, or patterns of messages, looking for evidence of international crime, terrorism, or anything suspicious.

Deep within the complex, on one of the many screens, an operator noticed a very unusual signal. It had a peculiar *zigzag* pattern and was quite unlike anything that he had ever seen before. He called over his section leader, who was equally as confused by what they were seeing.

Both men also felt a headache in their temples, which had suddenly appeared, apparently from nowhere, just like the signal.

What had started out as a usual shift was now rapidly changing. They both felt quite ill, and had trouble focussing, feeling quite faint, as the unusual signal merged with the very unusual sensation. It felt as though something was messing with their minds, and it was as though they had somehow been asleep, and were now waking up.

They felt different, and as they looked around the room, they noticed that everyone else seemed to be suffering from the same symptoms. People were holding their heads, and looking confused, and one of their superiors came into the room, and stumbled almost losing his balance.

He wanted to know what was happening, and had already sounded the alarm, sending the whole base into a panic. People were running about outside, all going to their emergency positions, getting ready for whatever they were going to face.

The unidentified signal was causing havoc with everyone, and head aches, dizziness and a general feeling of unreality was commonplace.

Back inside the control centre, the man at the screen desperately tried to compose himself. He had a job to do, and the years of training kicked in as he tried to identify where the signal was coming from.

Thankfully his mind soon began to clear, as the headache eased. He still felt confused, realising that he had not been himself for several weeks. He looked at the date on the top of his shift log, wondering if there had been a mistake. The last thing he remembered was crunching through the frost, and yet it was now summer.

His mind seemed to have a void where spring should have been, and he was not on his own, as everyone in the room seemed to be having the same thought. His superior officer was looking at his watch, scratching his head in disbelief. The date seemed all wrong, as it was three days after his wife's birthday, and he had an awful thought that he had forgotten all about it.

When he checked with the nearest shift log, he could not believe his eyes, he was not three days late, but *three months!*

That was not the only unusual thing to be going on, as the operator discovered. When he isolated the signal, he discovered that it had originated from GCHQ!


The faintest smell of gun power drifted across the room, so faint that it was almost impossible to detect, as the sound of the revolver being fired reverberated around the room. It was quickly followed by the sound of someone falling to the ground, and the three women gasped, not daring to open their eyes.

Everything seemed to have gone wrong for them, and now it appeared that the man at the centre of their thoughts was now dead. That feeling remained with them as the sound of a second body hitting the floor startled them.

They quickly opened their eyes, hoping that some sort of a miracle had taken place, and were astonished to see the Professor standing there unharmed. At his feet lay the two suited men, who were writhing on the floor, with a large black rabbit sitting by them.

Oracle had jumped out of the escape hatch in his bag, and had fired his taser, just as the older suited man fired. Looking across they could see the bullet hole in the wall, and the gun was now lying on the floor at Sagittarius's feet.

The security men had not moved, both holding their heads, and looking dazed. Even Sagittarius was not sure what had just happened, as he had expected to die, and yet had been saved.

"Blast!"

The older suited man cursed, having been foiled again!

Oracle still had him covered, and was deciding whether to shoot him again. The younger suited man also looked shocked, quite literally as it turned out!

Sagittarius calmly bent down recovering the revolver and handing it to Captain Charlotte, who took it off him, looking into his big brown eyes.

Two sets of blue eyes also looked up towards him, and all of them wanted to put their arms around him, grateful that he was still alive. They all remained seated, however, still unsure as to whether they would ever be forgiven for what they had done?

The security men were in pain, having suddenly developed blinding head aches. They felt confused, dizzy and nauseous, and had difficulty standing. It was as though their brains were about to explode, and neither of them could fathom out what was going on. For some reason they had no recollection as to why they were standing there, or who the other people in the room were. The last thing that they remembered was starting their shift, and that seemed like months ago!

Whilst they were standing there, the door suddenly burst open and in rushed four armed soldiers and an army Colonel. The sight of them seemed just as baffling as what they were doing there, and even though they tried to react, for some reason their bodies refused to move.

Instinctively, Captain Charlotte got to her feet, saluting the Colonel, followed by Gemini and Caprica, despite the fact that neither of them were real soldiers.

"Thank goodness you're still alive!"

The Colonel spoke as the other soldiers secured the room.

"I feared that we would not make it in time - a bit of a dash from the barracks, what!"

He then saluted the three women, before announcing to Sagittarius who he was.

"Colonel Mustarde, S.I.G."

Sagittarius put his head in his hands - of all the names that he could have had, it would have to have been *Mustarde*!

His mind instantly thought of the childhood board game Cludo, and that combined with Captain Charlotte or *Scarlet;* someone, somewhere must be sitting on a cloud having a good belly laugh at his expense.

The chances of just one of them having a surname like that was slim, but for both of them to have them, the odds must have been astronomical. The whole situation seemed ludicrous, particularly when there was a group of devious individuals who were intent on not only controlling the country, but practically halving the entire population too!

"The SIS building is now secure, and thanks to your efforts, we are now in the process of retaking GCHQ."

Sagittarius looked at him in amazement, having believed that his mission had failed.

"I don't know how you managed to block the signal to those satellites, but whatever you did, it seems to have worked."

He looked at the Colonel in amazement.

"Splendid job, Professor!"

Sagittarius looked at the others, who all shrugged their shoulders, equally as bemused as he was.

"It was a near run thing you know."

There was only one other explanation, and as he looked down towards his feet, there was Oracle sitting on his hind legs. He looked up at Sagittarius and twitched his whiskers nonchalantly, and as he sat there, a mischievous grin spread across his face.

"So, are we in the clear then?"

The Colonel nodded.

"Yes, Agent Bond has retaken the SIS building, and the Government is now free from control as well."

That was another pleasant surprise, although with a Special Agent going by the name of *Bond, Jayne Bond*, he began to wonder how he had got mixed up in all of this.

"You look a little lost for words, Professor."

That was an understatement!

One minute he was facing almost certain death, and the next he had been liberated. That was not the only shock that he had had, as when he had looked down at Oracle, he had given him a mischievous grin. Something very strange had been going on!

"Why don't you let me buy you a drink, and I can explain everything."

The Colonel's offer seemed like the best idea anyone had had for what seemed like a quite a considerable time. He certainly needed a drink, and a stiff one at that!

"I would love to."

Sagittarius gratefully accepted, and got up off the chair, looking back towards the three women. They just smiled, half expecting him to ask them to join him. He was tempted, but after what had happened in the main computer room, he decided against it.

The Colonel left the soldiers in charge, as they made their way towards the door.

"Extraordinary turn of events don't you think, Professor?"

Sagittarius nodded, still in shock.

"I must admit that I find the whole thing very disturbing, and to think of how close they came to actually pulling it off."

He breathed out, opening his eyes widely.

"We must make sure that nothing like this ever happens again!"

He would have no arguments from Sagittarius, who would be glad to get back to some sort of normality.

Fortunately, the nearest café was only a short walk away from the tunnel, and Sagittarius used the time to clear his mind. It had been quite an ordeal, and one which he never wanted to go through ever again!

It was the same café he had visited earlier, and the effeminate man was still serving. He recognised Sagittarius, and winked suggestively at him, as he stood next to the Colonel. The Colonel did not seem too impressed, and looked back at Sagittarius, who shrugged his shoulders. Maybe there was something wrong with his pheromones?

The café was virtually deserted, and they sat at the same table he had sat at before. Why did everything he did seem to have a touch of déjà vu about it?

With a great deal of relief, he took a sip from his fruit juice, as the Colonel poured himself a cup of tea from the stainless steel tea pot. He did not mind the smell of tea that much, and was thankful that it was not coffee!

"Now then, Professor, I'm sure that you would like me to fill you in on what has been going on."

Sagittarius just sat there, feeling a bit dazed by it all. Life had seemed so simple when he had just been *Head of Experimental Department.*

"I am sure that you are aware of the Secret Intelligence Service *SIS*, more commonly known as *MI6* or *Military Intelligence Section 6*, which is the British agency that supplies the British Government with foreign and home intelligence."

Well, he had been a member for several years!

"As you know, it operates under the formal direction of the Joint Intelligence Committee *JIC* alongside the Internal Security Service *MI5*, the Government Communications Headquarters *GCHQ* and the Defence Intelligence *DI*. Its headquarters has been at the *SIS building* on the South Bank of the River Thames since 1995."

Again, Sagittarius knew this and nodded.

"The existence of *MI6* was not officially acknowledged until 1994. In late 2010, the Head of *SIS* delivered what he said was the first public address by a serving Chief of the Agency in its 101-year history. His remarks primarily focused on the relationship between the need for secrecy and the goal of maintaining security within Britain. He acknowledged the tensions caused by secrecy in an era of leaks and pressure for ever-greater disclosure."

Sagittarius wondered where he was going with this?

"The main reason for making the statement was not to allay public fears, but to alert them that something was wrong."

Sagittarius already knew from his own experiences, that things were not right, and the fact that virtually the whole Agency had been compromised.

"More than a decade ago, a few of us became concerned by the behaviour of some of our colleagues, and this concern began to grow. We became increasingly concerned, as it seemed as though there was an *outside influence* as it were *pulling the strings.*"

This was information that he knew only too well!

"Every day, it seemed as though more of the Agency was falling under the control of this *outside influence*, so much so that we felt that it was only a matter of time before the whole Agency was compromised."

Sagittarius took another sip of his fruit juice.

"There seemed to be only a handful of us who remained outside of this control, and so we formed a secret counter group

146

within the Agency, alongside some of our foreign allies. It was now not a matter of one country against another, but those few who remained *loyal* to their own governments working together."

He did not like where this was leading.

"We knew that you were considered to be a bit of a *maverick*, and that you were working secretly on something. Our hope was to persuade you to join us, but before we could make contact with you, the Organisation got to you first."

Sagittarius opened his eyes widely.

"You were our last hope, as we were convinced that whatever you had been secretly working on would be the decisive factor, and whoever had access to it would eventually win."

Sagittarius remained silent, as some of the pieces started to fit together.

"Alarm bells rang as our plans began to unravel, and if it had not been for our agent *Dark Star*, then we would have surely failed."

That name sounded ominous, and Sagittarius had a bad feeling about it. Just the mention of that name made his heart sink, as he wondered where this *Agent* fitted into the equation. The Colonel could see the look on his face, and realised that Sagittarius was suspicious.

"*Dark Star* is a computer expert, and was recruited by the Organisation to coordinate the nano technology and link it to the satellite system. Our agent was in fact a *double agent*, and somebody who had worked for us in the past. Now, I'm sure that you still have a few doubts."

147

He was certainly right about that!

"Therefore, there is only one way in which I can convince you that I am telling the truth."

Sagittarius did have his doubts, not only about *Dark Star,* but about the Colonel too. He had learnt over the past few days not to trust anyone, and wondered what he was going to do next?

"So, I would like to present you with none other than *Dark Star.*"

The door of the café opened, and out from the kitchen walked the infamous person code-named *Dark Star.*"

Sagittarius could not believe who was standing in front of him, for there was Big Jim, with a big beaming smile on his face.

"Dad!"

"Son!"

They both embraced.

"You did not honestly think that I took early retirement did you?"

Sagittarius did not know what to think.

"Things were getting serious and, as you know, I had my concerns. I really wanted to tell you, but we felt that you needed to remain in the *dark,* so to speak. I was working undercover, with everyone naturally assuming that I was some sort of an eccentric old hippie."

That was still true, as he did fit that description!

"The stakes were high, and I knew that I could not just ask you to hand over all of your research, we also needed to *flush out* some of the Organisation's operatives. Once we did this, we were able to infiltrate the Organisation to a greater extent."

He looked at his father realising that he had been used as bait.

"I'm sorry son, but there was no other way."

Sagittarius was not very happy about that!

"The Organisation seemed to have *tentacles* everywhere, and they almost managed to achieve what they had set out to do."

That was all very well, but he had been shot, held prisoner several times, injected with foreign nano robots on more than one occasion, and had quite a traumatic experience overall.

Somehow, he could not fully believe that his father would have put him in so much danger.

"The Organisation is vast, and even now, we have only just scratched the surface."

Sagittarius frowned. All that effort and yet it was just a minor victory. Or was it, he was still not quite sure?

"Does my mother know about it?"

Big Jim shook his head.

"No, I managed to hide it all from her too!"

Sagittarius opened his eyes widely. His mother Astrid was a psychic, and had been married to Big Jim for over forty years. There was no way that Big Jim could hide anything from her.

"It must have been difficult."

Big Jim smiled, or was it a smirk?

Sagittarius looked at the Colonel, nodding towards his revolver, and raised his eyebrows. The Colonel understood

149

what he meant, and not quite knowing what he was up to, he handed it over.

Sagittarius pointed the gun at his father's head.

"I do not believe you!"

Big Jim looked amazed.

"What are you doing - I am your father!"

Sagittarius looked straight into his eyes.

"There is no way you could hide anything from my mother!"

The Colonel looked astonished.

"Who are you?"

Big Jim held out his arms.

"I am your father!"

"Oh no you're not!"

Sagittarius could see his tongue moving within his mouth, and quickly slapped him hard on the back of his head with his free hand.

A small brown rubber sphere, about the size of a small pea shot out, bouncing off the table, onto the floor and shattering releasing a liquid.

"Potassium cyanide!"

The Colonel looked flabbergasted.

"This is not my father, and you were right when you said that *Dark Star* was a double agent, unfortunately he has been working for the wrong side!"

"Well, bless my soul!"

The Colonel suddenly realised that he had been fooled.

"Good work, Professor!"

"He could never have fooled my mother, and he not only gave himself away by trying to pretend that he had, but my father never smirks!"

The other Big Jim looked very angry.

"They probably managed to get hold of my father's brain wave patterns whilst he was doing his research. They no doubt got hold of a whole a lot more besides. This is a *doppelgänger*, surgically altered and programmed to resemble my father."

The Colonel looked astonished.

"Is that possible, another one?"

"Yes Colonel, I'm afraid that you have been deceived!"

The Colonel shook his head.

"The devious swines!"

"At least you now have the opportunity to interrogate him."

The Colonel was very thankful. They now had both of the suited men, Taurus, the Doctor, and probably several others too in custody, and would be able to gain a lot more information about the *Organisation.*

"There have been discussions within the *S.I.G.* about offering you a permanent position. I can see now that we have made the right decision!"

Sagittarius could see the logic, but if this was going to be the sort of thing that he had to deal with, then his first instinct was to refuse.

"We would like you leave the Experimental Department, and take charge of what we term as *Mysteries*."

He enjoyed dabbling with new inventions, and the Experimental Department had provided him with the opportunity to complete Oracle.

"I'm not sure."

Sagittarius looked thoughtful.

"Anything unusual that we encounter, we would like you to investigate, and there will be far less paperwork than you have been used too."

That was the one thing that did get him down about his current job, together with the cutbacks, which were making it more difficult to get the raw materials or funding for any new projects.

"Obviously there would be a substantial increase in salary, and far less restrictions than you are used to now."

There was his disciplinary hearing to consider too, although that had proved to be another attempt to remove him by the Organisation.

The Colonel was dangling quite an interesting *carrot!*

The *stick* however, was something that he had already encountered, and he needed to have some more information about it before he made his decision.

"You do not have to make your mind up now, why don't you take some time off to think things over?"

Now that seemed like an excellent idea!

# Twenty One

The sunlight glistened off the calm waters of the Mediterranean sea, which sparkled like the lights of a Christmas tree as the yacht cut through the gentle spray. The warm gentle breeze ruffled its sails as it made its way towards one of the small islands that lay just over the horizon. This was indeed the calm after the storm!

Sagittarius began to relax, with nothing more to worry about apart from gently tacking into the wind. The yacht had its own motors, so there was no need to use the sails, although they added to the feeling of *oneness* with the world. It was more than capable of accommodating at least ten people, although on this particular journey he was travelling alone, apart that was from his trusted friend and companion Oracle.

He would never be able to thank his father enough for allowing him to use his two weeks of the time share, or for all of the help and support that he had given. Who would have thought that he had also been copied, and that there had been another Big Jim, posing as *Dark Star*.

It had been quite a revelation, and one that had come as quite a shock. Life was full of surprises, and he now realised that the Organisation had spent several years using his research for its own devious means. It had been a brilliant plan, and one which had almost succeeded. If he had not spotted the fact that the *doppelgänger* was not his father, then they would have had someone on the *inside* capable of turning everything back in their favour.

Big Jim had been horrified when he had been informed, and after the initial shock, had accepted the offer to become a member of *S.I.G.* himself. Together they had helped to save the

153

Nation, if not the World, from the grip of those dreadful power crazed individuals, and he grimaced when he thought about how close they had actually come to success.

Sagittarius knew that his father would never have used him in such a manner, and placed his only son in such danger. How many others had they copied, and just how far did the tentacles of the Organisation really stretch?

It did not bear thinking about, and he tried to place the thought to the back of his mind.

The soothing sound of classical music gently played from the radio as he let his thoughts drift away, thankful that it did not contain the *bellowing* and *warbling* of operatic singers. Fortunately, it was not too heavy either, as the last thing he wished for was mournful violins, or hammered piano keys that would have grated on his ears.

Sagittarius was not much of a classical music lover, but every now and again he liked to relax with something soothing such as a gentle waltz. It seemed appropriate as the yacht danced through the waves, and he began to hum gently to himself.

The waltz finished and there was the unmistakeable sound of the bleeps signalling the hour, followed by the time, and then the news headlines.

*The Government has announced that the so called 'Bat Flu' pandemic has been downgraded as a result of new information. All restrictions were lifted earlier today, and the inoculation program has been cancelled.*

*The Prime Minister has been criticised for overreacting to the situation, and will face a grilling in Parliament from the opposition leader later today.*

*A Government spokesman has also stated that there is now no danger to the public as the virulent strain predicted has failed to materialise.*

*All borders have reopened, and travel restrictions lifted, and it is hoped that things will be back to normal by the end of the week.*

Sagittarius smiled to himself, as he knew the real reason behind the announcement.

*The Army has been recalled, and all Police leave has been reinstated. We are now going over to our Chief Political Correspondent for a special report.*

*Today saw a humiliating climbdown by the Prime Minister, which has left his credibility and competence in question. However, it is doubtful whether he will face a vote of no confidence. If that was to take place, then in theory it could trigger a general election.*

Sagittarius turned off the radio, not wishing to hear any more about it. He knew the truth, and the idea of his holiday was to get away from it all. That was not the only thing that he was trying to get away from!

There had been three very attractive young women, who had tried to force themselves on him, and he cringed when he thought about it. Under normal circumstances he would have been flattered, and maybe something could have developed in time. He was however a one-woman man, even though he found relationships rather difficult.

The sight of three of them fighting over him had been far too much for him to bear, as their hormones had gotten the better of them.

155

But having said that, he did have quite a lot to thank Gemini, Caprica and Captain Charlotte for, although he felt sure that they understood his need to be alone. He knew that the two young women would be safe enough with his parents, and now that they had regained a lot more of their faculties, they were no longer so dependant on him. The Captain also had to return to her regiment, and he was relieved that there was not going to be a repeat of their performance.

Relationships, particularly with women, did not come easily to him, being a bit of a loner. He had been in love once, but after the breakup of that relationship, he had vowed never to be hurt again!

It had taken him quite a while to get over it, and in some ways it still hurt. People always say that you remember your first love, and he still did. They had met at university, and were both still young, and on reflection maybe they had not been ready for such an intense relationship. It had been wonderful whilst it lasted, but as soon as they had graduated, everything seemed to fall apart. He had been glad of his parents' support at the time, and now even though he was staunchly independent, their help and support had saved him again.

He was so grateful for having such wonderful parents, always so kind and caring - a little too caring sometimes!

All of their love, affection and support had been gratefully received, and had given him a firm foundation upon which to build his life. He knew that all they really wanted for him was to find love and happiness, and had raised their hopes when he had arrived at their home with Gemini and Caprica.

They were always there to encourage, and push him towards any women they felt was suitable, and on this occasion having two of them had not changed anything. Whether it was one, two or even three, he doubted whether they would raise an eyebrow, as long as whoever he was with made him happy.

It was a little strange having a couple of ageing hippies for parents, and their belief in peace and love remained. The prospect of his father becoming a *Special Agent*, made him smile. Who would have thought that a *conspiracy theorist* would now be working for the *Secret Service*. It was a brilliant cover, and Big Jim was the last person that you would have ever expected for the job.

He had been given some time to repair *Freedom Farm*, and there was now added security in place. The *bunker* had been fortified, and the *lads* were now also officially *Special Agents*. That made him smile again; who would have ever believed that Britain's first line of defence would have been ten black *stealth rabbits*!

Thinking of stealth rabbits…

One thing that he really needed to do was to give Oracle a good overhauling. He had seemed to have developed a personality, and it did not appear to be an entirely good one at that!

He was almost like a teenager, and it had come as quite a shock to discover that his creation had begun to develop anything in the way of individual thought, let alone a personality. He was supposed to be just a machine, a *cyber rabbit* which was going to be nothing more than a computer on four legs with a few added gadgets.

They shared the same memories and experiences, and he guessed that in some ways they were very much alike. Now that he had discovered emotions, he had opened up a virtual

157

*Pandora's Box.* However, having started to develop a personality of his own, he still had an awful lot to learn.

Human emotions were very complicated things for most people to deal with, and now that they were being experienced by a *machine*, it could lead to all sorts of problems. Oracle was now beginning to show signs of behaviour like a *naughty teenager*, especially as he had begun to learn all about *hormones.* It was his fault that the three women had acted the way they had, although Oracle had kept a lot of things quiet!

Big Jim had also played a part in his creation, and perhaps that was where he got his mischievous nature from?

His father had quite a sense of humour, a big *cuddly teddy bear* of a man who everyone seemed to like. He was always up to something, some secret venture or surprise. Being a *Special Agent* was going to be the biggest secret of them all, and he wondered how his mother was going to cope with it?

He could not keep anything from her, particularly with her intuition and psychic abilities. The more that he thought about it, the more he wondered what the future would bring for them?

However, it did not seem to matter what his father did, as they had been virtually inseparable for their entire adult lives. They had always been so happy together, and the main thing was that they had managed to defeat the Organisation on this occasion, although there was always the distinct possibility that they would try again.

That was not his concern, as he was going to forget all about them and enjoy his holiday.

He breathed in the sea air, letting it fill his lungs, as all thoughts of Organisation left him with his exhaled breath.

He, like his father, loved to sail, and it had been rather fortuitous that two weeks had become available just as the pandemic ended!

It was even more fortuitous that a private jet had been chartered, courtesy of *Her Majesties Secret Service*. In these days of austerity, it was something which he had never expected. That, and the fact that there had been no one there to wave him off. Gemini and Caprica had taken the news really well, a little too well now that he thought about it!

They had clung onto him like *limpets*, not letting him out of their sight, and yet, they had not been there when he left. Thinking about it, he suspected that Oracle had a lot to do with that too. After all, he had reprogrammed them, and been playing with their oestrogen levels.

Sagittarius had also noticed that he had developed what amounted to a mischievous grin, although at first he thought that he had been imagining things. How could a *cyber rabbit* have such a thing?

He looked over towards him, and Oracle looked back, and there it was again!

This was very odd, and perhaps there was some sort of a *glitch* in his programming?

He seemed to be operating well enough, so it was nothing to worry about. When he got back, he would certainly run a full diagnostic on him, just to make sure that he was not going to get out of control!

The wind rustled through the sails as he eased the helm into the wind again, with the yacht groaning slightly, making a few sounds just like most houses do at night. His home was no

159

exception, and being quite an old property, it did tend to creak from time to time. He was not thinking about going home yet though, as he had his whole holiday in front of him to look forward too. It had been very kind of his father to go on ahead, and sort out all the supplies. He had assured him that he would have everything he needed for a holiday of a lifetime. Now that he came to think about it, Big Jim had the same mischievous grin on his face as Oracle!

Sagittarius had been so keen to get under way that he had not even checked the store compartment, which was a little careless of him. He just assumed that his father had provided everything he would need, and now that he came to think about it, he could do with a drink. There did not seem to be any other boats in the area, so maybe in a few minutes he would lock the helm and venture back to the stern, to see what he could find.

With his mind wondering, he suddenly felt two sets of arms grab hold of him. Sagittarius froze, with the sudden thought that the Organisation had not finished with him yet. He had put the groan of the ship down to the wind, but now he realised that it must have been the sound of intruders!

His heart sank, as he envisioned two men dressed in black combat gear, and anticipated the sharp prod of a revolver in his side.

Everything went into slow motion, as he did feel something.

It was a kiss on both cheeks, and as he looked round, there were Gemini and Caprica wearing the smallest bikinis that he had ever seen!

No wonder they had let him go so easily!

It looked as though he was not going to enjoy a quiet relaxing holiday on his own after all!

Nothing was said as they just smiled at him, contented that they had their man just where they wanted him!

He then felt the warm embrace of two sets of arms holding him around the chest, stroking the hair which protruded from his muscular torso. They did not seem to mind his age, and he had to admit that he was in rather good condition for a man in his forties.

He gave the helm a slight turn, making the muscles of his powerful legs ripple under his white shorts, following the navigation system, as he corrected course. It was then that he felt another set of arms slipping around him, followed by another kiss. This one was on his neck, and the arms gently pulled him away from the helm.

They slid him around, and as the lips found his, there standing in front of him was Captain Charlotte, also wearing a minuscule bikini which showed off her very ample curves!

The kiss was very passionate, and nearly took his breath away, and as they slid apart, he only had the one thought on his mind.

Oracle!

Oracle sat there with the wind in his ears, looking for all the world like a very spoilt pet rabbit on his holidays. There were certainly no other rabbits in existence who had experienced such an adventure, real or cyber!

He turned his head around, sensing that Sagittarius was looking at him, and as he did so, he gave the biggest mischievous grim that he had ever seen!

Oracle then turned his head back to face the sea, and with his ears still flapping in the breeze, they all sailed off towards the horizon…

# Thank you for reading my book

If you enjoyed this read, please leave a review on Amazon. It only takes a few minutes and it really does make a difference.

Just click here to go to my author's page.

At the side of the title click on see more, and scroll down until you see customer reviews

Click on write a customer review and click on the stars

Thank you so much!

# Free Book

Thank you for downloading this book.

Your purchase also entitles you to a free book!

A Way of Being - The Journey to Spiritual Enlightenment

A spiritual awakening with a little angelic guidance…

This book introduces the reader to the subject of angels. It is also a semi-autobiography which details how the author became an angel artist.

Angels are there to guide us and help us on our life's path, and to open up a doorway to the spirit world. Beautifully illustrated it is an ideal companion for the Angel Intuition/Colour Therapy card deck, which is available separately.

Revised edition!

Available in ebook format usually priced at £1.99

**For your free copy please click on the link below**

www.ingramcontent.com/pod-product-compliance
Lightning Source LLC
Chambersburg PA
CBHW070926130626
46555CB00001B/297